St. Mary's Church, Iffley Village

The Recluse of Iffley Village

By

Emily Beaver

The Recluse of Iffley Village
Copyright © 2008 by Emily Beaver
Meriwether Mystery Series

Original Illustrations by A.J. Beaver

All rights reserved. No part of the work may be reproduced or transmitted in any form or by any means, electronic or mechanical, including photocopying, recording, scanning or otherwise, or by any storage or retrieval system, except as may be expressly permitted by the 1976 Copyright Act, or in writing from the author.

Requests for permission should be made in writing to:

Smooth Sailing Press
Attn: Publisher
PO Box 1439 / Tomball, Texas 77377
9306 Max Conrad Drive / Suite C / Spring, Texas 77379

Printed in China

ISBN 978-1-933660-42-4

SMOOTH SAILING PRESS
(281) 251-0830 / www.smoothsailingpress.com

St. Mary's Church, Iffley Village

The Recluse of Iffley Village

By

Emily Beaver

The Recluse of Iffley Village
Copyright © 2008 by Emily Beaver
Meriwether Mystery Series

Original Illustrations by A.J. Beaver

All rights reserved. No part of the work may be reproduced or transmitted in any form or by any means, electronic or mechanical, including photocopying, recording, scanning or otherwise, or by any storage or retrieval system, except as may be expressly permitted by the 1976 Copyright Act, or in writing from the author.

Requests for permission should be made in writing to:

Smooth Sailing Press
Attn: Publisher
PO Box 1439 / Tomball, Texas 77377
9306 Max Conrad Drive / Suite C / Spring, Texas 77379

Printed in China

ISBN 978-1-933660-42-4

SMOOTH SAILING PRESS
(281) 251-0830 / www.smoothsailingpress.com

This book is dedicated to my sisters –

Joellen, who helped me remember

and to Lila, who read my book!

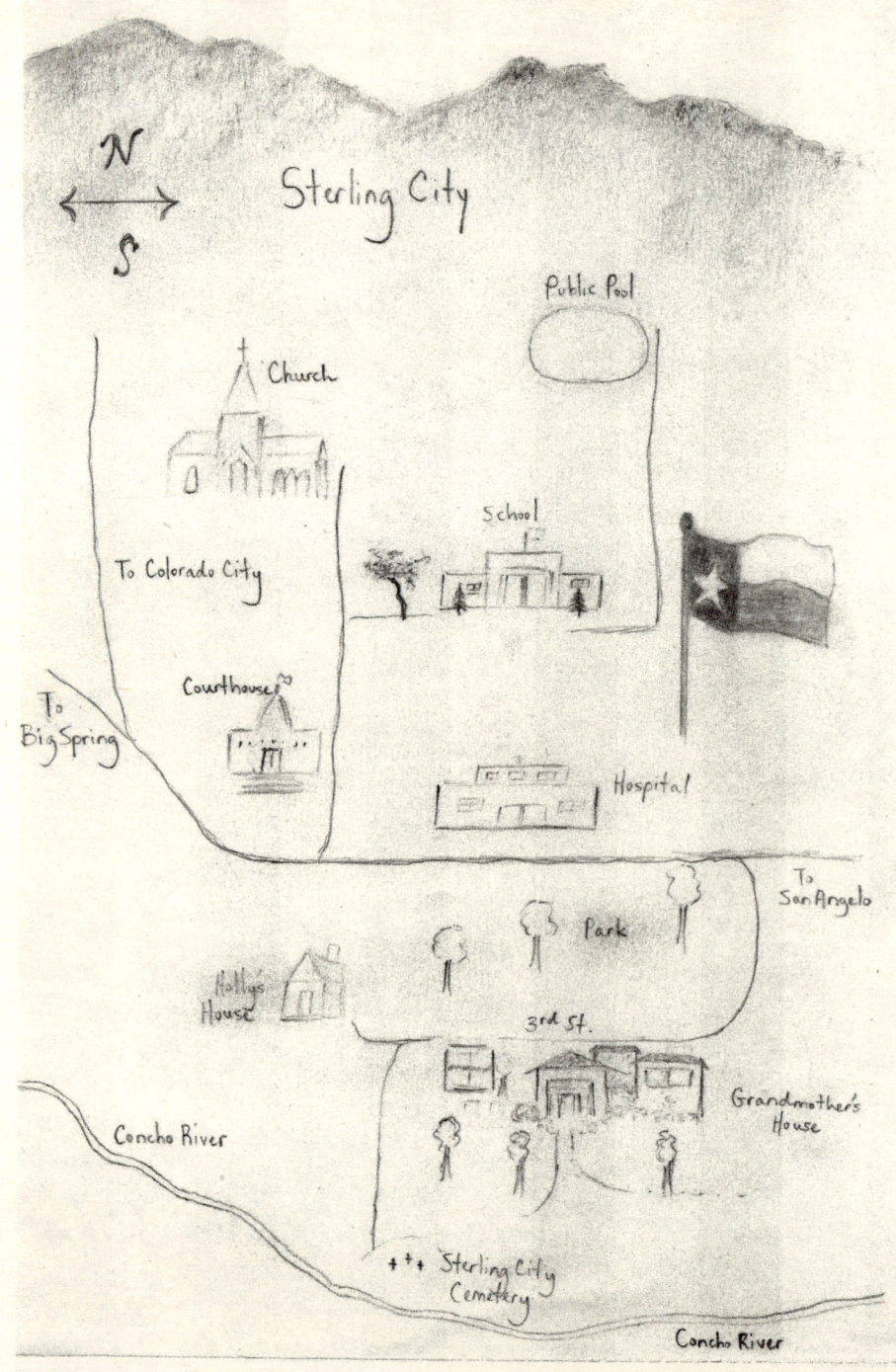

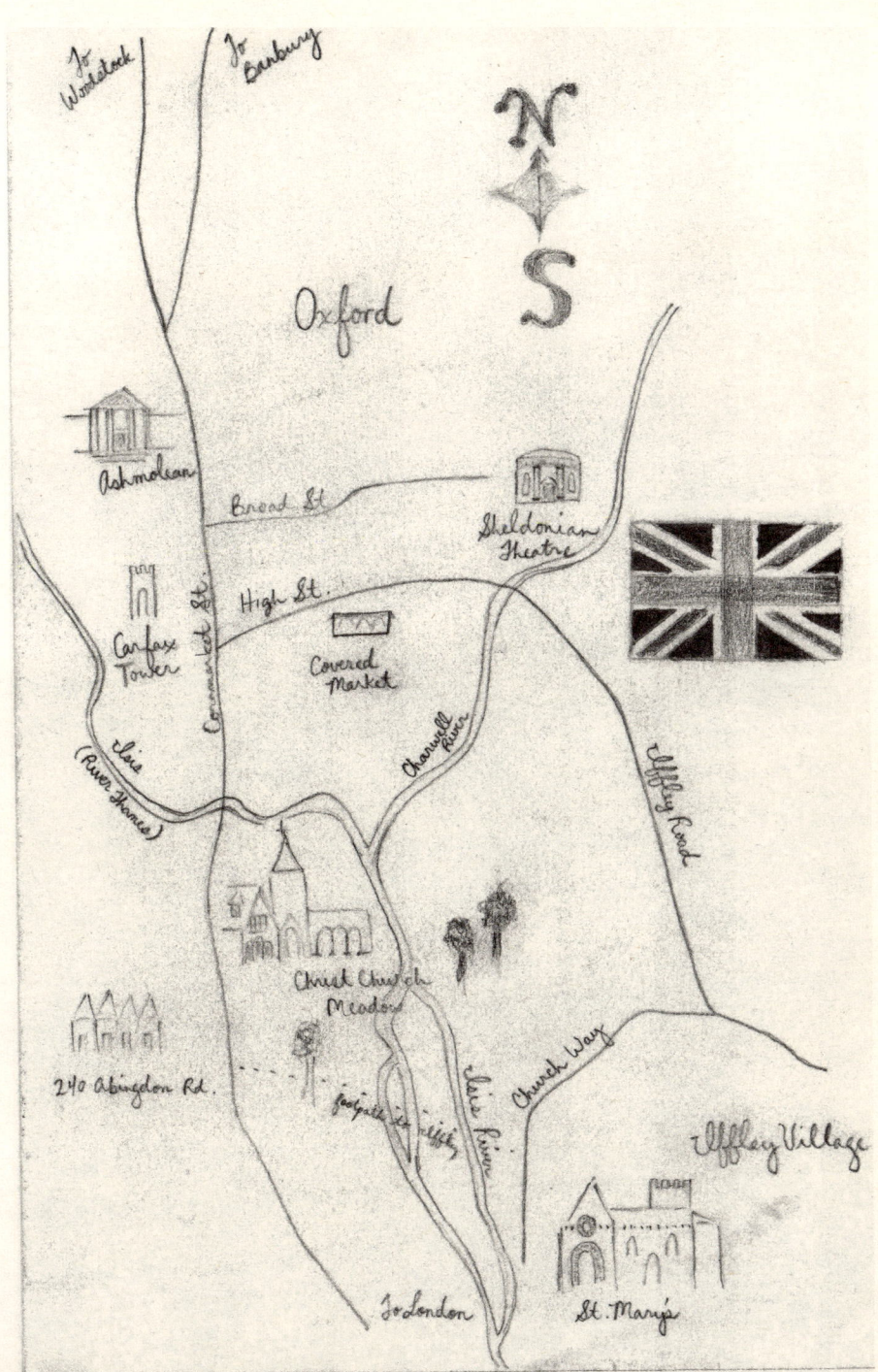

Meriwether Mystery   Emily Beaver

Chapter One

Meriwether awoke to the happy sound of birds chip-chirruping outside her bedroom window. A ray of sunshine peered through a crack in the curtains, illuminating a corner of the quilted comforter folded neatly at the end of her bed.

She immediately knew something was wrong.

It wasn't that the house was too quiet. It was always quiet, unless Maricella was there running the vacuum. It wasn't anything she could put her finger on exactly. She just knew.

Rubbing sleep out of her eyes, she squinted at her watch: 8:30. *Strange*, she thought. Grandmother never allowed her to sleep past 8:00. Meriwether threw the covers off, dressed quickly in white cotton shorts and a sleeveless coral polo, and pulled her wavy hair into a ponytail.

Grandmother did not condone walking around the house in one's pajamas.

Down the hall which housed the family photos; through the den where Grandmother would sit and read and where the two of them would watch television at night; across the large tiled sunroom with its wall of windows that gazed out onto the flagstone patio, perfectly

Meriwether Mystery Emily Beaver

manicured lawn, and tennis court beyond; and into the breakfast room - which was where she should be . . . drinking a cup of coffee and working the word jumble in the newspaper - 'to keep her mind sharp.' But she wasn't there.

Maybe she's outside, thought Meriwether, inexplicable fingers of dread reaching up into her throat. *This is ridiculous,* she told herself. *Get a grip! She's just gardening before it gets too hot.*

From the window lined breakfast area, French doors opened onto a fountained courtyard. Meriwether poked her head out and called, "Grandmother?" -- No answer. A quick round about the perimeter of the house proved that she was not outside.

What if she's sick in bed, Meriwether thought suddenly, *too sick to get up?*

She raced back through the house, turned right at the hall, and knocked gently on Grandmother's part-way open door. "Grandmother?"

Meriwether pushed open the bedroom door to find a perfectly made bed. *Okay, just breathe,* she reminded herself. *She's here somewhere.*

Meriwether tip-toed through the silent bedroom, stopping at the entrance to Grandmother's mirrored and closeted dressing area and put her ear to the pulled pocket door. "Grandmother?" she called tentatively.

Straining, she imagined she could detect the slightest sound of shallow breathing issuing from behind the door.

Sliding the door back an inch, she whispered, "Grandmother, are you okay?"

No answer. But now Meriwether was certain of that

same belabored breathing.

Panic rose up in Meriwether like a wave, crushing all sense of caution.

She threw open the door ...Grandmother, her face a grayish-green mask of fatigue and pain, lay crouched in the corner of her dressing room. Her spectacles were askew, and a fine coat of perspiration covered her pallid features. Her left hand gingerly cradled the opposite wrist, and both arms were pulled close to her chest.

Meriwether stood rooted to the spot. She could not take it all in. Instead of going to her grandmother, she stared stupidly at the cracked and splintered glass about two feet above where Grandmother now slumped.

Grandmother lifted her head heavily, her glazed eyes finding Meriwether and struggling to focus on her. "Call . . . an . . . ambulance . . ." she managed before losing consciousness.

Meriwether Mystery　Emily Beaver

Chapter Two

Meriwether sat in the hospital waiting room, absentmindedly fingering the white piping of the vinyl settee her legs were sticking to. A travel magazine lay open in her lap to an article about Stonehenge. Normally, Meriwether would have been very keen to read an article about Stonehenge, but today there was only room in her mind for one thing: that horrible image of her capable and stately grandmother . . . in pain . . . helpless.

After fumbling to make the necessary call, Meriwether had ridden along in the ambulance to the small community hospital. One of the responding paramedics had put his big, dark arm around her shoulders and reassured a white and shaking 'Miss Meriwether' that Grandmother was going to be all right.

But Meriwether was not so sure, and even though she knew he was just trying to make her feel better, did not appreciate the sentiment. How did he know Grandmother would be okay? Was he a doctor?

Grandmother had never been sick a day in her life, that Meriwether could remember. 'I'm as healthy as a horse!' Meriwether had heard her say on more than one occasion. She could hardly bear to think of Grandmother altered . . . or worse.

4

Meriwether Mystery   Emily Beaver

The waiting room doors separated and in rushed Holly, Meriwether's best friend, and Holly's father, Mr. Hart, the editor of the local newspaper. Holly was athletically slim and taller than Meriwether, which wasn't saying much because Meriwether had always been small for her age; her tanned skin and long blonde hair contrasted dramatically with Meriwether's own fair complexion and unruly chestnut locks.

Dark blue eyes wide as saucers, Holly spouted, "Mrs. Rodriquez just called the house maybe ten minutes ago to tell Daddy what happened! Mom said you're to come to our house tonight and for as long as you want, and I told Daddy I was coming with him whether he liked it or not, and he said okay, but I had to get dressed -- we were still eating breakfast. So I did, and here we are!"

At this point, Holly paused for breath and Mr. Hart sat down beside Meriwether and patted her knee, "Meriwether, are you all right? How about a coke? You look like you could use something in you."

"Yes, thanks," muttered Meriwether, trying very hard not to cry. So far, she'd gotten away with not having to say anything. Somehow, opening her mouth made it much harder to keep her emotions under control.

"Good, I'll be right back," smiled Mr. Hart, producing a neatly ironed and folded handkerchief. Meriwether pressed the handkerchief to her face. She could still detect the fresh smell of detergent, and it helped her feel better.

"Mer, are you really okay?" asked Holly softly, crunching into the settee beside her friend. "Mrs. Rodriquez told Daddy that you were the one who found her. That must have been just awful!"

"Yeah, it was awful . . . and, yeah, I'm okay." Meriwether forced the image of her grandmother out of her mind.

"How long have you been here?"

"Um," hesitated Meriwether, glancing at the large clock positioned over Mrs. Rodriquez's reception desk, "about an hour, I guess. . . wish I knew what was going on in there. Thanks for coming."

"Sure! Remember when John broke his collar bone last year? We sat up here for hours with that one. And I always have to come visit my Auntie Esther in the nursing home. I don't like hospitals . . . but I hate the nursing home. At least at the hospital it's, you know . . . temporary. The nursing home is so final . . . and horrible," she ended with a small shudder.

Meriwether knew exactly what she meant. Granddaddy had been in the nursing home at the very end, when he got so bad that he could no longer be taken care of at home. Meriwether had been five years old, and that was the only time she had ever seen a crack in Grandmother's armor -- until today. *The funeral was also the last time I saw my dad*, the thought came unbidden and she pushed it away just as quickly.

"Here you go," said Mr. Hart, arriving just in time with a soda. He knelt down beside Meriwether, put his hand on her knee, and said in a low voice, "I saw Dr. Swann in the hall. Meriwether, your grandmother had a heart attack. She's just out of surgery and in the recovery room...They'll move her to a private room when she's ready ...I'm so sorry," his hand patted her knee methodically.

Meriwether felt her insides turn to ice. This was bad. Really bad.

Holly wrapped her arms around Meriwether, who sat there stonily, staring into nothing.

"Doc told us to go on home," continued Mr. Hart softly. "Your aunt is on her way. They'll call us if there is any change at all.

"Let's go back to the house and see what Carol and the boys are up to. We'll come back up here tomorrow to visit your grandmother."

Meriwether nodded absently, and allowed herself to be directed out of the hospital. Mr. and Mrs. Hart and Aunt Phil would take care of everything. Grandmother would be okay . . . she had to be.

"Carol said she would go over to the house and get some of your things," said Mr. Hart as they crawled into the seen better days station wagon. "Anything she leaves out you can borrow of Holly's."

"Thank you," replied Meriwether robotically, but inside she was thinking, "Thank goodness!" The idea of walking back through the house after the ordeal of the morning made her positively goose pimply.

"It *is* a horrible thing to have happened, and don't think for a minute I'm glad about it," gushed Holly, "but this is going to be so much fun! I hope you get to stay with us all summer! What do you say, Daddy? Wouldn't that be fun! Mom said she could stay as long as she likes, and," focusing her attention on Meriwether, "Well? Don't you *want* to stay with us?"

"What? . . . Oh . . . yes," responded Meriwether, forcing herself to concentrate, "I mean . . . if it's okay," she added, looking nervously at Mr. Hart.

"It's fine with me, girls, . . . and I'm sure Carol will have no objections . . ." replied Mr. Hart cautiously, "but I think we'd better wait until we see Mrs. Knight tomorrow before making any long term plans."

"Oh, it will be fine," whispered Holly, rolling her eyes. "What do you want to do first?"

'First' turned into a game of PIG with Luke and John, Holly's brothers. Luke, the older of the two, at seventeen, was big and strapping with light brown hair and a smile for everybody. Sixteen year old John was more reserved and not quite as strapping, but his athleticism equaled his brother's, even if his shoulder width did not. He was taller and had blonde hair like his sister.

PIG consisted of basketball shots made from various positions on the court, or driveway, as the case may be. First player up shot the ball. If the ball went in, the next player had to attempt the basket in the same way from the same place. For instance, Luke had a signature shot: a one-handed spin shot from the free-throw line that he made about 80% of the time. Successful completion on Luke's part would invariably result in a P, I, or G for the next player. The first person to spell PIG or, in effect, miss three baskets that the player before had completed, lost; but the game was typically played until last man out.

Luke and John let Holly and Meriwether play, but the real competition was between the boys. Even so, Meriwether was having a great time, despite occasional feelings of guilt for completely forgetting about her grandmother for whole minutes at a time. She always had fun at the Hart's. It was so different from her own home. The Hart family was big and buoyant and even a little chaotic, and the most splendid part about it was that nobody seemed to mind.

"Lunch!" called Mrs. Hart from out the kitchen

Meriwether Mystery   Emily Beaver

window. "Ya'll come on in!"

"I've fried up some ham, and there's corn on the cob, and a jello salad," chattered Carol Hart as she ushered them into the kitchen a few minutes later. "Hands washed?" she demanded of her children as they exchanged looks of mock irritation.

"Come on Mom, we're not preschoolers," complained Luke.

"Well then, are they washed?" replied Mrs. Hart, eyeing him suspiciously.

"Okay, okay! We give up! Come on, John," and the two stamped good-naturedly to the sink.

"Hands clean and ready for inspection, sir!" barked Holly with a quick salute, a self-satisfied grin spread across her face.

"M-hm, Meriwether is a very good influence on you. Always said so, haven't I Martin?" Mrs. Hart smiled back, winking at her husband.

"Yes, and you're absolutely right. Maybe Meriwether's presence in this house will teach our thundering herd a few manners," answered Mr. Hart in good fun.

After lunch, the girls went for a swim at the pool. By the afternoon, of course, the entire town had heard about Mrs. Knight, and everyone was very solicitous, asking after her . . . if there was anything they could do. Meriwether didn't know what to say but tried her best to be polite.

By the time they got back to the Hart's, Meriwether's aunt had called to report on Mrs. Knight. Her condition was stable, thank God.

For supper, they ordered pizza -- lots of pizza -- from

the diner and watched a movie. They'd all seen it before, but it was a family favorite; and that night, Meriwether crawled into Holly's trundle bed, exhausted. She closed her weighty eyelids only vaguely dreading tomorrow's visit to the hospital.

"G'night, Mer."

"G'night, Holly."

Meriwether's reservations about visiting her grandmother in the hospital were two in part. First, and foremost, she did not want to see Grandmother dressed in a hospital gown and looking the part of an invalid.

What's more, Aunt Phil was there.

Grandmother and Aunt Phil loved each other, but they did not get along. They both wanted to be the boss.

Each time Aunt Phil came to visit, she would spend the whole time pointing out places Maricella should be cleaning and things Meriwether should not be doing. This drove Grandmother, who took great pride in her superbly run home, close to the brink. Most times, she would end up saying something sharp and hurting Aunt Phil's feelings so badly that it would be several weeks before they were forced to endure another visit.

More than anything, Meriwether was terrified Aunt Phil would suggest that Meriwether return home with her until Grandmother was fully recuperated.

Aunt Phil did not approve of the Harts. Aunt Phil commanded a very tight ship and kept her one husband, two children, and three Yorkshire terriers in line at all times. She knew everyone's schedule down to the minute: where they were, who they were with, and where they were going next.

Grandmother, who was very strict about

Meriwether's behavior inside their home, trusted Meriwether with her own business when she was out of it. Although her freedom was nothing in comparison to Holly's, it was enormous compared with her two unfortunate cousins. Surely Grandmother knew Meriwether would rather stay, if necessary, with the Harts and that they were happy to have her. Surely, even if Aunt Phil suggested it, Grandmother wouldn't make her go.

Chapter Three

After a raucous and frenzied breakfast next morning, a frazzled Mrs. Hart, blonde hair pulled haphazardly into a top knot . . . little tendrils escaping and curling from the heat of the kitchen, announced it was time to go to the hospital. Luke and John headed off for baseball practice, while Mr. and Mrs. Hart, Holly, and Meriwether piled into the station wagon.

When they got to the hospital, the three Harts stayed in the waiting room while Mrs. Rodriguez escorted Meriwether to her grandmother's room. Meriwether took a deep breath, steeling herself for whatever she would find inside, and knocked lightly on the door.

"Come in!" answered a firm, familiar voice, and Meriwether's initial fears were immediately put to rest. There was her grandmother, sitting ramrod straight in the hospital bed, attired in her own lavender dressing gown and plum colored house shoes. Her right arm was in a sling, injured when she collapsed, but her waved silver hair looked as if it had just been to the hair dressers. A pair of hip, jade green reading glasses rode low on her prominent nose.

Mrs. Knight removed her glasses and set them down on the newspaper she had been reading. Meriwether

Meriwether Mystery Emily Beaver

walked to the left side of the bed and placed her hand in Grandmother's substantial free one.

"Help me finish the word jumbles." Grandmother, not one for sentimentality, was down to business. "I've already figured the first ones out. I just need you to write them in for me and then we can get the daily riddle. I'm too old to learn to write with my left hand."

Meriwether dutifully obeyed, pulling up a chair and gathering up the newspaper and a nearby pencil. The first word was RTWAHT. Meriwether unfocused her eyes and let the letters swim before her mind, rearranging them at will until they formed a word: thwart.

She was already filling in the circles as Grandmother said, "The first word is 'thwart.'"
When completed, the word jumbles looked like:
    RTWAHT - THW<u>A</u>RT
    TYHWSRA - S<u>WA</u>RTHY
    UCLAIRC - <u>C</u>RUCIAL
    AKMRTE - MAR<u>K</u>ET
    POCUTOS - OCT<u>O</u>PUS

"Now we have to unscramble the underlined letters to give us the answer to the daily riddle," said Grandmother. "I've already got it. Let's see what you can do with it."

The daily riddle read, "What every witch wants: Her _ _ _ _ _ _ _." Meriwether once again allowed her eyes to unfocus, letting the letters form into the word she wanted. Grandmother nodded approvingly as, after only a few seconds, Meriwether wrote in "warlock."

"You have your father's mind," remarked Grandmother, "and he has mine." Then, after the few seconds of deafening silence that followed the

13

Meriwether Mystery   Emily Beaver

unaccustomed compliment and mention of her father, "Philomena has invited you to stay with her family while I am recovering. Dr. Swann says six weeks of rest at the least, but maybe longer for an old woman like me."

Meriwether's mind was reeling, "No! No! No!" But instead she said as calmly as possible, "Holly's family has invited me to stay with them. They said they'd be happy to have me all summer. They're in the waiting room if you want to talk to them," she added hopefully.

"I'm afraid all summer is much too long to impose on anyone outside of the family. It was very kind of them to offer . . . but it's impossible," answered Grandmother.

"But . . . ," attempted Meriwether.

"No buts," replied Grandmother firmly. Then in a kinder tone, "Don't worry. I have no intention of making you stay with Philomena. I have made other plans for you." Meriwether's emotions were roller-coastering about so quickly that she hardly had time to wonder **what plans?** before her grandmother continued, "I've spoken with your father, and he has agreed to have you for the summer. You will leave sometime next week. Philomena is making the arrangements and will drive you to the airport."

There seemed no room for argument. Grandmother had it all figured out. Meriwether's mind was fit to burst with,

    1.) Disappointment - she would have had such fun with Holly,
    2.) Relief - at least she wasn't doomed to spend the summer with Aunt Phil,
    3.) Excitement - she was going to England!
    4.) Confusion - why, after almost twelve years of barely speaking her father's name, had her

grandmother decided to send her to him? And why, after almost twelve years of virtually ignoring her existence, had her father agreed to have her come?

In a daze, Meriwether replied, "Yes, ma'am," as a gentle knock sounded from the door.

"May we come in?" Carol Hart peered cautiously around the partially open door.

"Yes, yes. Come in!" answered Fiona Knight as Mr. and Mrs. Hart and Holly filed into the room.

"I've made you some of my banana nut bread, Mrs. Knight," said Mrs. Hart, setting a foil wrapped loaf on a table piled high with potted plants, flower arrangements, and fruit baskets. "I know how much you like it."

"Thank you," smiled Mrs. Knight, "and thank you for taking care of Meriwether. I'm sure I gave her quite a fright yesterday."

"No problem at all," replied Mr. Hart. "We were glad to have her, and we'll be happy to keep her for as long as you need to get back on your feet again."

"All summer is no problem!" added Holly, and then, "Gosh, Mrs. Knight, you look great for someone in the hospital!"

Mrs. Hart shot a stern look at her daughter, but Mrs. Knight just smiled, "Thank you, Holly. Dee came by to fix my hair first thing this morning, and Philomena went to the house and brought me some of my own things. She's gone back to town to make arrangements for Meriwether's trip, but she'll be back this afternoon with Roger and the children," at this point, an almost imperceptible frown flitted across her face.

"Her trip?" echoed Holly.

"Yes, you see I'm afraid we will have to decline your generous offer to take Meriwether in. She will be spending the summer with her father in Oxford," replied Mrs. Knight.

"You lucky dog!" squealed Holly as she grabbed Meriwether up in a massive squeeze. "What I wouldn't give to go with you!" Her excitement seemed genuine; no trace of disappointment was discernable on her smiling face. Meriwether decided to share her enthusiasm.

"Yeah, can you believe it?" she smiled, hugging Holly back.

"Philomena will drive her to the airport early next week," continued Meriwether's grandmother, "but if you would be so kind as to keep her with you until that time . . ."

"Of course we will!" answered Mrs. Hart without hesitation.

"Well then, it's settled," said Mrs. Knight, "and now, if you don't mind, I think I need a nap. Come back and see me before you leave, Meriwether."

"I'll come every day, to help you with the word jumbles," replied Meriwether.

"Very well, then . . . tomorrow . . ." and her eyes closed as her head rested against the pillows.

Chapter Four

    The week with Holly and the Hart family went by in a flash. Meriwether was good to her word and rode her bike to the hospital every day. The accident had occurred on a Monday, and on Friday Dr. Swann released Mrs. Knight to the care of Philomena. Philomena would stay with her mother through the weekend and then take Meriwether to the airport on the following Monday. After that, Aunt Phil would return home to her own family, and Maricella, who was unmarried, would come to live in the big house with Grandmother.

    After church on Sunday, and a pot-luck dinner afterwards in the fellowship hall, Meriwether said goodbye to Holly and her family and returned to the only home she had ever known.

    Meriwether's English mother had died soon after her birth. As an infant, Meriwether had been delivered from England to be raised by her grandparents. Meriwether had received, by mail, a birthday gift on June 25 and a Christmas present on December 25 - strange and unusual gifts - for the past eleven years.

    She had met her father only once: at Granddaddy's funeral nearly seven years ago. There were portraits of her father, as a child, hanging in the hall. Awards and trophies he had won for sports or stock showing was displayed in the trophy case in the den . . . but his name was almost never spoken. Meriwether tried to remember what he'd looked like, but all her mind could conjure was very tall and very sad.

Aunt Phil helped Meriwether to pack, which was difficult because neither one of them knew what to expect from the weather. It could never be as hot as a West Texas summer. It might even get chilly -- and would probably be wet. In the end, they packed some of everything, and Grandmother lent Meriwether a credit card with strict warnings to use it only if absolutely necessary.

Through all of this, Meriwether realized that Aunt Phil did not approve of Grandmother's decision to send her to her father's.

"Of course I haven't seen him in years," prattled Aunt Phil, "but I hope he at least remembers you're even there. He can be very forgetful . . . especially when he's working ...Well; you know that you can always call me if it gets too bad. I'll arrange for you to come straight home."

This dreary prediction did nothing to relieve the knot in Meriwether's stomach, which had been tying itself since Grandmother's announcement over a week ago. And what was that Aunt Phil had said about, 'when he's working?' What did her father do, exactly? No one had ever thought to tell her, and for some reason she didn't dare to ask.

That night, Meriwether went to Grandmother's room to say goodnight and goodbye. She and Aunt Phil would be leaving at 6:00 the next morning to make a noon flight leaving from Dallas/Ft. Worth airport, with a short stopover at Chicago O'Hare, then on to London/Gatwick where her father was to meet her some 13 hours later. Grandmother motioned for Meriwether to sit down on the edge of her bed. She seemed different somehow -- frailer, and older.

"Are you ready?" she asked as Meriwether placed her hand inside her grandmother's. "Do you have your birth certificate?"

"Yes, ma'am," answered Meriwether, trying desperately not to cry.

"I asked Maricella to find this for me today," said Grandmother, taking a long, thin gold chain from around her neck. On the chain hung a small, golden key. "Wear this around your neck. Do not take it off. When you get to Oxford, give this key to Peter."

"Yes, ma'am," replied Meriwether, mystified, as she took the chain from her grandmother and put it around her neck.

"Do not forget . . . And do not forget that I love you."

" . . . I love you too."

It was the first time they had ever spoken those words to one another.

Meriwether Mystery Emily Beaver

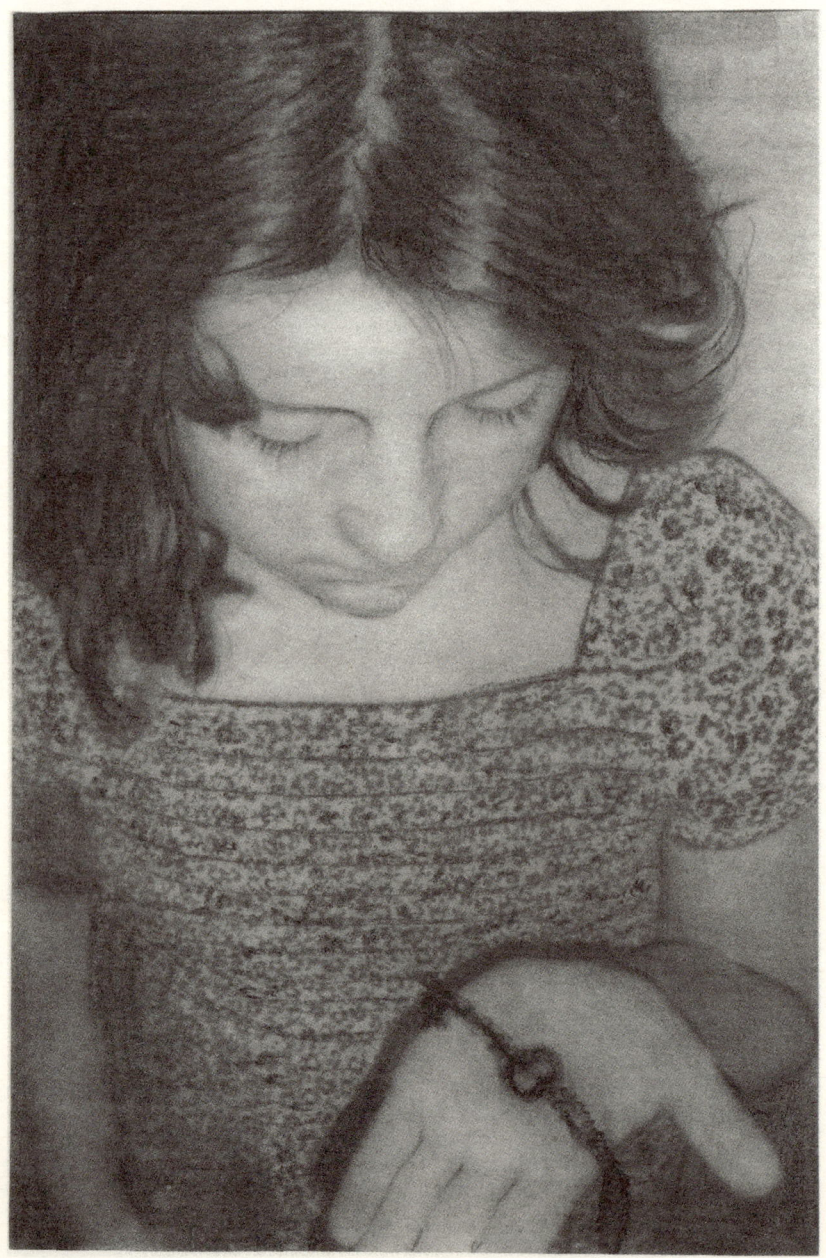

Chapter Five

Meriwether slept fitfully through the night; so, being very tired next morning, she spent a good part of the drive catching up on her rest. At odd intervals she would wake up and surreptitiously check the chain she had carefully concealed beneath her T-shirt and denim jacket. She couldn't really explain this need for secrecy except for the fact that Aunt Phil noticed everything and was sure to ask questions about the chain, and especially the key, if Meriwether allowed her to see them. The only thing Meriwether knew was that it seemed very important to Grandmother that her son, Meriwether's father, be given that key. *Why?* was one of the things that had kept her awake most of the night.

At intervals, Meriwether watched the terrain shift from wild, sun-burnt pasture to the gently rolling grassy hills and fields of Central Texas. Soon enough, all she could see from any direction were the buildings and billboards, traffic and super highways that made up the Dallas/Ft. Worth metroplex.

Bustling through the airport, Aunt Phil made up for lost time by offering a thousand and one helpful hints for international travel . . . such as, "When you get there, no matter how tired you are, do not go to sleep until ***their*** bed time. If you do, you'll be off schedule for heaven knows how long."

Truly, a fate worse than death, thought Meriwether wryly.

And, "Eat a little of whatever you're offered, just to be polite, but I wouldn't expect much. The British are notorious for their bland foods."

And, "Try to stay away from public bathrooms."

Finally, Meriwether was hugging her aunt goodbye and hoisting her backpack, which she would be using as a carry-on, onto her shoulder. This was not her first plane flight, but it was the first one she could remember. She was not nervous about flying; on the contrary, she was very excited. So excited, in fact, that she could not seem to keep her mind on one thing for more than a few seconds. She pulled out an interesting looking autobiography that she had found in Grandmother's library at home - but could read no more than a few pages. Even her favorite mystery, which she had also brought (even though she had already read it twice), could not hold her attention today. Instead, she gave up on reading and turned her attention to her fellow passengers.

She noticed a young Middle Eastern woman sitting across the aisle and one row up. Tall and slim, her long, jet black hair was fashioned into a braid that fell midway down her back. Dressed in an ivory linen pant suit and gold hoop earrings, a discreet pair of rimless reading glasses perched on the end of her nose, she perused the pages of a black leather folder with the words Poole & Assoc. engraved in gold leaf on the binding. Meriwether fancied her a lawyer, on her way to research a big case.

A little boy with a teddy bear sat straight across

from her, hunched down in the window seat. She had seen him at the airport, clinging to his mother. They had both been crying. Maybe he was going to see his dad too.

A small man with thinning grayish hair and a haggard, sallow complexion inhabited the row behind Meriwether and to her left. He wore a cheap, rumpled suit, and, once, when Meriwether turned to look at him, he was looking back at her. Embarrassed, she gave a quick smile, but he looked away almost immediately and began to type away on his lap-top. Meriwether imagined he was some sort of business man, very much in need of a vacation.

"I hate to fly, don't you," chatted Meriwether's next seat neighbor, a friendly older woman with an English accent, as they munched a lunch of dry ham and cheese sandwiches, potato chips, and limp pickle. Meriwether's mouth was full of sandwich, so she could not respond beyond putting the tips of her fingers to her mouth to show she was still chewing and to please give her a minute - but it seemed no response was necessary. "I didn't want to bother you earlier because I saw you were trying to read. I just hate it when people try to talk to me when I'm reading! But I noticed you put your books away, and now that we're eating lunch, I thought, *surely she wouldn't mind a bit of conversation*. You don't mind, do you? A bit of conversation, I mean."

"No," replied Meriwether, trying not to giggle, "I don't mind."

"Well, good! That's what I hate about flying, you know. No one to talk to for hours at a time! It's dreadful, and I find that if I stay bottled up for too long, I simply can't stop myself when I get home, and I'm afraid my poor

Tom isn't what you'd call a conversationalist. Very dissatisfying for both of us, if you know what I mean."

Meriwether smiled and nodded. She could just imagine 'poor Tom' enduring a barrage of bottled up babble. Stifling another giggle, Meriwether asked, "Do you travel often?"

"Well, that depends what you'd call often," replied Mrs. Poor Tom. "My daughter and her family live in Dallas. That's where I've been. I visit once a year and they come to us for Christmas. My sister's in Edinburgh and we get together as often as we can. My son and his family live in Bournton, same as Tom and me, so we see them all the time," she chattered. "And you, my dear? You seem awfully young to be traveling alone, though not as young as that poor lamb," nodding at the little boy curled up in his seat, lunch untouched.

"No, ma'am. This is my first trip. I've never been anywhere before . . . ." In fact, to date, nothing much had ever happened to Meriwether. Soon, Meriwether found herself telling friendly Mrs. Poor Tom all about Grandmother's accident and the unprecedented decision to send her to her father's. She told her about her mother's death and being sent to Texas to be raised by her grandparents. She even told her about the inscrutable key and instructions Grandmother had given her, and they both wondered about it.

By the time they had arrived in Chicago, Meriwether and Mrs. Poor Tom, (a.k.a. Rosemary Shockley), had become fast friends, and Meriwether and her father had received an open invitation to visit the Shockleys at their farm in Bournton, *a lovely little village in the Cotswolds.*

"Ladies and gentlemen, I'd like to welcome you to Chicago, the Windy City," the captain's voice droned from the intercom.

"You're on to London then?" confirmed Mrs. Shockley.

"Yes," Meriwether nodded.

"Well then, stick with me, dear. We'll find our gate together."

"Thank you," replied Meriwether, very grateful indeed that she would not have to navigate O'Hare alone.

There was a huge bustle to get out of the plane, and then the passengers dispersed in a hundred different directions. Meriwether saw the young boy, escorted by a flight attendant, run to greet his dad with a leap and a huge bear hug. They both seemed very happy, and Meriwether was heartened. She only hoped that her own reunion with her father would be half as joyous.

"Boarding rows 15-30, to London Gatwick. Rows 15-30, flight 315 to London Gatwick, boarding now," announced a flight attendant.

"This is it," puffed Mrs. Shockley as she fished out an embroidered handkerchief from her large handbag and dabbed at her face and neck, "and we've just made it. They're already boarding, and that's me: seat 17F," she panted, fumbling with her boarding pass.

"Thank you, Mrs. P . . . Mrs. Shockley. I never would have made it without you."

"There, there dear," answered Mrs. Shockley, pressing her warm, soft cheek against Meriwether's. "Now don't forget to come and visit. I simply must hear how it all turns out! The answer to your mystery! We'll be expecting you anytime." And then she added, "You know, I have a feeling that you are going to have a grand adventure!"

Meriwether smiled and waved as Mrs. Shockley disappeared down the boarding tunnel, directly behind the Middle Eastern woman and the rumpled man with the computer from the previous flight.

"Yes," thought the newly optimistic Meriwether. "I have the very same feeling," and she boarded the plane anticipating the *grand adventure* awaiting her across the sea.

Meriwether's international flight was quite dull by comparison. She was seated beside a honeymooning couple who had eyes and ears only for each other. Every once in a while, she would glance back several rows and receive a wink or a thumbs up from Mrs. Shockley, who was talking animatedly with her new neighbor . . . good news for Mr. Shockley. But Meriwether didn't mind the solitude. She watched the in-flight movie, nibbled at her Salisbury Steak dinner, and then settled down to reading her mystery for the third time.

A few times she had the odd feeling that someone was watching her, but when she looked up -- nothing. She supposed that one of the passengers was people watching, just as she had done.

I wonder what they think about me, she thought to herself. Finally, as the airliner flew into darkness, Meriwether nodded off into a restless sleep, plagued by semi-conscious images of, among other things, mysterious keys and Aunt Phil making a next to impossible spin shot.

Several hours later, she was awoken by a flight attendant asking her to please return her seat to the upright position as the captain was preparing for descent.

Meriwether Mystery Emily Beaver

Her heart did a funny leap, and all of a sudden she felt like she was going to be sick.

Would she recognize her dad? Would he recognize her? What would they talk about? Would he like her? Would she like him? She took several deep breaths to calm her nerves. *Just relax*, she told herself and spent the next few minutes trying to make herself as presentable as possible, her hands shaking slightly.

A few minutes later, Meriwether was hoisting her backpack over her shoulder and being herded out of the plane. She waded through customs, showing her birth certificate in lieu of a passport - there hadn't been time to get one. She folded the certificate and put it in her jeans pocket, stepping out into the main terminal. A sea of people swam before her eyes. She scanned the faces, trying to find one that seemed familiar. There was Mrs. Shockley, hugging what must have been Mr. Shockley. The dark woman's cheek was being kissed by a very handsome, well-dressed man with a head full of snow white hair and blue, blue eyes the color of sky. The gray man had not been greeted by anyone but was heading off on his own. Still, no one came forward to meet Meriwether, and she could not see anyone who resembled the picture she had in her mind of her father. A terrible thought crossed her mind, *What if he forgot?*

Hadn't Aunt Phil warned her that her father was forgetful? What would she do? Her mind was playing out scenarios of spending the night, curled up in a chair at the airport, when she felt a touch on her elbow, "Meriwether Knight?"

She turned around, expecting to see her father, but, instead, there stood a boy of about 14, with reddish-gold hair, twinkling brown eyes, and a wide, easy smile. "Thought that was you," he said, sticking out his hand. "I'm Daniel Pleasant. Me gran looks after your dad," he added, seeing the look of puzzlement on Meriwether's face.

Regaining her composure, Meriwether smiled and returned the handshake, a nice firm one. "Hello, it's nice to meet you, Daniel." And looking around one more time, "Did you come with him? Where is he?"

Daniel shifted his feet uncomfortably and became very interested in a piece of thread coming loose from a buttonhole in his jacket, "No, um, see your dad, well, he asked me to come fetch you for him. He had somethin' important he had to finish up."

Meriwether was deeply disappointed, but she didn't want Daniel to know it. "You came by yourself?" she asked incredulously.

"Oh, sure!" he piped, relieved that he was not going to have to comfort a crying little girl -- the picture he had been drawing in his mind up to that point. "I come to London all the time to run a quick errand or two for Gran or for me mum," he explained as he led Meriwether to the baggage claim area.

"These are mine," said Meriwether, reaching out for her bags as they came round on the conveyor belt.

"I've got it." Daniel stepped in front of her, hefting one bag over his shoulder and lifting the other with his free arm. He flashed the mischievous grin, "Ready, then?"

"I've already checked, and the coach to Oxford doesn't leave for another hour," Daniel explained as they made their way through the airport. "Are you hungry?"

"Starved," Meriwether stated truthfully.

"What'd you get on the plane?" asked Daniel.

"Salisbury Steak," Meriwether replied with a small grimace, laughing at the expression of disgust etched across Daniel's face.

"Right, then. We'd best get a bite first. No time to leave the airport, but" . . . he continued, scanning the many shops and restaurants, "yeah, here we go. You like hamburgers?"

"Yeah, sure," nodded Meriwether. "Um, should I get some money changed over or something?"

"No need. Your dad gave me some pounds for the train, but this'll be my treat."

"That's okay, you don't need to spend your own money," hesitated Meriwether.

"Just say,' Thank you, Daniel,' and you can return the favor once you get yours all sorted out," he grinned.

"Thank you, Daniel," Meriwether conceded as she returned his contagious smile.

Not exactly the first meal she had anticipated eating in England -- a burger and fries had never tasted better. Daniel was easy to talk to, completely at ease with himself and, Meriwether imagined, any situation he happened to find himself in. It was not until they rose to make their way to the coach station that Meriwether realized her backpack was missing.

"It's gone!" exclaimed Meriwether, searching frantically behind her chair, under the table, beneath her tray.

"What's gone?" asked Daniel.

"My backpack!" cried Meriwether. "I set it down right here," indicating the floor in back of her chair, "and now it's gone!"

"When's the last time you saw it?" Daniel asked

29

Meriwether Mystery Emily Beaver

calmly.

Meriwether thought for a moment and then answered, "I guess it was when you went up to the counter to order our food. I put it down and haven't looked back since."

"That must have been when it happened," said Daniel. "I would have noticed, otherwise."

"That must have been when what happened?" wondered Meriwether dumbly.

"Someone nabbed it, obviously," he explained. "Anything important in there?"

"Not really," Meriwether made a mental list of the backpack's contents. "Just some books, a $20 bill, and a change of . . ." Meriwether had nearly said 'a change of underwear', but she quickly amended her answer, "clothes, in case my luggage got lost . . ., and my toothbrush." Thankfully, Grandmother's credit card and her only copy of her birth certificate were in the back pocket of her jeans, and the key, as a quick check confirmed, was still hanging safely around her neck.

"Well, there's no use looking for it or filing a report, then. Not much damage done. Congratulations, Meriwether!" smiled Daniel, patting Meriwether on the back. "You've just learned an important rule for survival in the big city: If you want to keep it, keep your eyes on it."

"No teacher like experience, I guess." Daniel's calmness, like his smile, was catching.

"Well done! No sense crying over spilt milk, that's what me gran always says," beamed Daniel, once again sincerely pleased to have avoided any waterworks.

"We can get you a new toothbrush in here," said Daniel, pulling her into a nearby souvenir shop. "Anything

30

else you need?"

Meriwether had done her best not to embarrass herself and keep up her end of the conversation, but by the time they boarded the coach, she was feeling brain tired. Daniel, seeming to sense that she needed some alone time, reclined his seat, folded his arms at his chest, and announced that he was going to take a nap.

"It's a straight shot to Oxford. Takes about an hour," and with that, he closed his eyes and fell instantly to sleep.

Meriwether didn't feel like sleeping, but she did need to think. She liked Daniel very much; in fact, she could only imagine Holly's reaction when she wrote to tell her about him, but Meriwether couldn't understand why her father had sent a 14 year old boy to meet the daughter he hadn't seen for seven years. Then, her grandmother's words came back to her, *I've spoken with your father, and he has agreed to have you for the summer.*

Meriwether knew how . . . *persuasive* her grandmother could be. What if he didn't want her here at all? What if he had merely said, *Yes*, to get Grandmother off his back? Was she to be ignored all summer, and was Daniel to be paid to amuse her? She immediately felt sorry for these thoughts. Daniel had been so kind, not at all like he had been forced to come or that he minded her company in any way. He had said that her father had to finish something up. That must be the 'work' Aunt Phil had been talking about. Meriwether's curiosity was on fire. There were so many things she didn't know about her father!

All of these thoughts raced through her mind at lightning speed, but as the coach pulled out of the station, and fields and countryside began to replace parking lots and buildings, all of her angst literally flew out the window her forehead was pressed against. *It's beautiful!* she thought, her heart singing. *I've never seen grass so green!*

Bits of villages flew by that Meriwether yearned to explore, and she knew that this was only the tip of the iceberg. She determined to see as many things and go as many places as possible, and if her father couldn't take her, then, hopefully, Daniel would do the honors. By the time they reached Oxford, she had pulled out the map Daniel had bought her at the souvenir shop and begun to plan her itinerary for the next six weeks. Despite the rocky start at the airport, an inexplicable feeling of belonging and familiarity began to fill her. In some strange way, Meriwether felt she had come home.

The coach began to slow. Daniel stirred, "All right?"

"Yes," replied Meriwether, folding up the map, "all right."

"We'll take a taxi to your dad's, and then we can go for a walk if you like," offered Daniel. "You've been sitting for an awfully long time. I'd be needing some exercise, I know that much."

"Thanks, yeah, I guess so," said Meriwether tentatively. A walk with Daniel sounded great, but she didn't want to commit herself, just in case her dad had something planned for the two of them to do.

Again, reading her thoughts, Daniel added, "Course, we'll see what your dad's got in mind, first. Let's just play it by ear."

Relieved, Meriwether replied, " Yeah, that sounds good ...Thanks, Daniel."

"Right-o," with a wink and a smile.

Meriwether Mystery   Emily Beaver

Chapter Six

Everything about the taxi ride to her father's house was fun. First of all, they were traveling down the wrong side of the road, and the driver and steering wheel were on the wrong side of the car! Daniel kept up a running commentary, pointing out various gray landmarks, "There's Carfax Tower. We'll climb up there one day and get a good view of the city. Down that way's the Sheldonian, can't see it from here, but Sir Christopher Wren built it in 16 . . . - What?"

"1667, I think it was," answered the wizened little man of indiscriminate age who was driving the taxi.

"1667. That sounds right," continued Daniel while the taxi eked around City Centre, zipping in little bursts of speed up St. Aldate's. "And here's Christ Church Cathedral. Beautiful, isn't it?"

Meriwether sat transfixed. She stared out the window, looking at everything Daniel pointed out, and more than once had to remind herself to close her gaping mouth. The history of the city was palpable, and Meriwether, who had never seen a building of more than 150 years in age, was in awe.

St. Aldate's presently turned into Abingdon Road. Rows of tightly packed brown brick town houses with

Meriwether Mystery   Emily Beaver

painted white trim lined the right side of the street, with adjacent views of green practice fields and the grounds of Christ Church College. The taxi made a U-turn and pulled up in front of one of the small brown houses, number 240. *This is it!* thought Meriwether.

Each time she received a gift from her father, the package would read:

```
P. Knight
240 Abingdon Rd.
Oxford, England
OX1-4SP


                    Meriwether Knight
                    #2 3rd Street
                    Sterling City, TX
                    76951
```

Daniel paid the taxi driver, whether with money Meriwether's father had given him or out of his own pocket she didn't know, and there they were, ringing the doorbell to the place she had wondered about for so long. She could hear footsteps coming down the hall, and before she knew it, the door was opened by a tiny little woman dressed in a pleated green cotton skirt and long-sleeved white blouse with a peter pan collar, a cameo pinned at her throat. Her fuzzy white hair made a halo about her face, lessening the severity of her dress, and bifocals hung by delicate chains against her chest.

When she saw her grandson, her lips spread into a familiar grin. "Good, good. I've been worried," she not so much said as sang in a lilting voice, thickly accented. Welsh, Daniel would later explain.

She ushered them into a tiny foyer with a boldly patterned kilim rug and antique umbrella stand. From the foyer, Meriwether could see a comfortable looking room with a fireplace and lots of books, and directly in front, down a short hall, the dining room and kitchen. A narrow staircase ascended to the upper floors, where Meriwether assumed the bedrooms must be. Everything seemed built on a curiously small scale, as if normal sized people could not possibly inhabit it.

"And this is the one we've been waiting so long for!" exclaimed Daniel's grandmother, taking both Meriwether's hands into her own. Meriwether could almost look her right in the eye.

"Sure, and don't you look like your mother," her eyes, scanning Meriwether's face, began to mist. A faraway look came over her and it felt to Meriwether as if she were not seeing *her* at all. Meriwether shivered involuntarily.

"It's all right, Gran," said Daniel softly, putting his hands on her shoulders.

"Yes, yes," answered Gran, releasing Meriwether's hands, pulling herself together. "Sorry, dear. Don't mind me."

"Meriwether, this is my gran, Effie Doone." Daniel stepped between the two of them, one of his hands on each of their shoulders.

"Hello, it's nice to meet you, Mrs. Doone," replied Meriwether dutifully, and then before she could stop

Meriwether Mystery   Emily Beaver

herself, "You knew my mother?" Meriwether had never heard anyone mention her mother before. Of course, she knew she'd had one, knew her name had been Felicia, knew she had died, but that was it. No one back home had told her anything about her mother because no one knew anything to tell.

"Oh yes, dear. Yes, I knew your mother," nodded Mrs. Doone. "Beautiful woman, inside and out, if you know what I mean. And I must say, the resemblance is striking."

"Do you, I mean . . ." Meriwether hesitated, "do you have a picture?"

"Of course!" Mrs. Doone motioned them to follow her into the cozy room with all the books. She led them to a large, leather topped desk and handed Meriwether a silver-framed photograph of a laughing woman with curling ash-blonde hair, fair skin, and a small, heart-shaped face.

"What color were her eyes?" asked Meriwether, mesmerized.

"The color of earth and water and fire," answered Mrs. Doone. "Just like yours."

At that moment, the telephone rang, and Mrs. Doone hurried to answer it. "Excuse me, dears."

"She's beautiful," breathed Meriwether, still holding the photograph, "and she looks so happy."

"Haven't you ever seen a picture of your mum before?" asked Daniel.

"No, never," answered Meriwether. "No one back home ever even met her, and I've only met my dad once, when I was five."

"Blimey, that's rough," commiserated Daniel. "No wonder!"

37

"No wonder what?" Meriwether was confused.

"Well, you're a trooper, that's all," Daniel shrugged. "Don't act like no eleven-year-old I've ever met."

"I'll be twelve in three weeks," retorted Meriwether quickly.

"Twelve then." Daniel's grin slid across his face, "Well, never mind. Very typical for twelve."

Meriwether knew he was making fun of her now, so she threw him a nasty look. All the same, she was flattered. She carefully placed the photograph back on her father's desk as Mrs. Doone came bustling back into the room.

"Well, and I've got bad news for you, as I'm sure you're anxious to see your father." A small frown creased Mrs. Doone's face. "That was his assistant, Gerry, on the telephone. Seems they need a few more hours . . . an important deadline to meet ...says Dr. Knight should be home in time for tea."

Muttering under her breath, she began to distractedly plump pillows on the sofa, a little more emphatically than was strictly necessary. "He hasn't seen his daughter in seven years ...important deadline ...hogwash! What's more important?"

Having taken her aggressions out on the pillows she again addressed the pair, "Daniel, be a dear and help Meriwether with her things while I make us a cup o' tea?" She turned on her heel and continued to mutter as she made her way to the kitchen, "Home for tea . . . he'd better be home for tea, if he knows what's good for him!"

"She likes you," smiled Daniel as he lifted Meriwether's suitcases. "After you," he nodded up the staircase.

Meriwether Mystery Emily Beaver

Meriwether's new room, a mere quarter of the size of her room at home, was papered with a fresh pink and white stripe and held a full-sized iron bed dressed in crisp white bedding. A marble-topped nightstand holding a Tiffany-style reading lamp and a vase of creamy peonies stood beside the bed. Gracing the far wall was an antique armoire with a mirrored front, and a fully furnished writing desk and chair were situated underneath the window that overlooked busy Abingdon Road below.

"Gran's been busy," whistled Daniel. "You should have seen this room a week ago!"

"It's perfect!" exclaimed Meriwether, hugging herself.

Daniel set down her bags and ducked out of the room. "Meet you downstairs in a bit."

"Thanks, Daniel . . . I'll just be a minute," replied Meriwether.

She fished in her suitcase for a hairbrush and some toothpaste, unwrapped her new toothbrush, and located the small bathroom right outside her doorway. Meriwether brushed her teeth, washed her hands and face with honey scented soap (the hot and cold water came out of two separate taps), brushed her hair and pulled it back into a pony-tail, and then headed back downstairs for 'a cup o' tea' with Daniel and Mrs. Doone.

Meriwether found them in the back of the kitchen conversing in low voices around a round wooden table, set against a bay window looking out onto the back garden.

"Oh, here you are dear." Mrs. Doone, immediately ending the conversation, jumped up and reached for the kettle that was simmering on the stove. "How do you take your tea?"

"I don't know," answered Meriwether. "I've never had hot tea before."

"Never had a cup o' tea!" exclaimed Mrs. Doone. "Well, we'll fix that. I'll make it like I do my own ...a bit of milk and a wee spoonful of sugar." Mrs. Doone busied herself with the tea. "There you are dear, a cup of tea and a warm scone, fresh from the oven."

"Thank you." Meriwether, who had never had a scone either, watched as Daniel plopped a large spoonful of strawberry preserves onto his plate and then slathered each bite with the fruit. She followed suit and was more than pleasantly surprised. Grandmother's idea of a midday snack was carrot sticks and raw broccoli spears. Holly would always insist they stop at her house first if they were on their way to Meriwether's after school.

"This is delicious, Mrs. Doone!" exclaimed Meriwether. "And thank you for my room. Daniel said you've put a lot of work into it."

"Don't mention it, dear. It was great fun, if you must know the truth. There are antique shops all over town, and I drive a hard bargain, if I do say so meself," she added with a mischievous wink. "If you need anything at all, you mustn't hesitate to let me know. Understood?"

"Yes, ma'am," replied Meriwether, wondering if Daniel had told her about the backpack and hoping he hadn't. "Thank you."

Mrs. Doone began to busy herself with cleaning up the plates and cups. "Daniel tells me the two of you have planned a walk. I'll expect you back, with time to spare, for tea at 6 o'clock. Off with you now! Have a good time!"

"Your gran is great!" chatted Meriwether happily as she and Daniel followed a small footpath through Christ Church Meadow. Green grass and tall trees surrounded them, effectively blocking out the sounds of traffic from the nearby street. Squirrels, accustomed to their human cohabitants, darted from tree to tree or hunched nearby nibbling a nutty snack.

"Yeah, she is. Thanks," responded Daniel. "Your dad's pretty great too, if you don't know."

"I **don't** know," said Meriwether flatly, "but I'm glad somebody thinks so."

"He just sort-of gets caught up in whatever he's doing," Daniel attempted to explain. "Gran says it's his artist's mentality."

Meriwether's ears pricked up. This was her chance to find out what her father really did! "So he's an artist? Your grandmother called him 'Dr. Knight.'"

"Well, yeah," answered Daniel, surprised that Meriwether obviously knew so little about her father. "He can do anything! He makes things in his shop, writes, takes pictures . . . but he works for the Ashmolean."

"The Ashmolean?"

"Our local museum. It's world famous, not just some rinky-dink thing," explained Daniel. "Your dad is an archaeologist, Meriwether ...specializes in restorations. He's all the time getting called to London to look at some Egyptian artifact or other."

Once again, Daniel's radar picked up Meriwether's weather pattern. "Don't worry, you'll get to know your dad soon enough. Bet he's got all sorts of plans for the two of you."

Meriwether smiled noncommittally. She wasn't so sure, but she knew Daniel meant it all for the best. To change the subject she asked, "So what does your dad do?"

"Don't got a dad," answered Daniel easily.

"I'm sorry." Meriwether could kick herself for being so insensitive. "Did he die?" she asked softly.

"Nah, he's not dead. Least I don't think he is. Left me mum before I was even born. Said he wasn't ready to be a dad. We think he's in America somewhere, but I've never laid eyes on the man." Daniel explained all this without missing a beat, but Meriwether thought she could detect some heavily veiled hurt lurking behind his deep brown eyes.

"I'm sorry, Daniel," Meriwether replied, carefully studying her shoes as they continued along the footpath. "That stinks."

"Yeah, well . . . it's okay. Mum's great. She works at a travel agency near City Center . . . and of course there's Gran. Your dad let's me come and go like I lived there, and I make some pocket money doing odd jobs for 'em. Can't complain!" Daniel's grin spread from ear to ear, "Want to cross over the river or keep going along this way?"

Meriwether looked up to find that they had come to a crossroads. The footpath continued off to the right, but almost directly in front of them curved a little wooden bridge which forded a narrow river. "Let's cross over."

"This here's the Isis, what we in Oxford call our part of the Thames. It widens up in a bit," Daniel explained.

And sure enough, the river began to expand in front of their eyes. They could see several small boats out on the water, and a couple across the river laying on a blanket and enjoying the warm afternoon sun. Daniel and Meriwether walked on for some time, enjoying a comfortable silence. After a while, they came to a larger bridge and crossed back over, which put them close to City Center and High Street.

"Want to see the Covered Market?" asked Daniel.

"Sure!" answered Meriwether, who was not used to so much walking and was beginning to wonder how long it would take to get back to her father's house. She checked her watch, which she had already set ahead, "I guess we have time."

"Don't worry," Daniel noticed the quick look at her watch. "We'll take the bus back. I've got a pass. We'll need to get one for you soon. You'll like the Covered Market. Bet you've never seen anything like it."

And indeed, Meriwether hadn't. It was like a mall and a grocery store rolled all into one. Butcher shops with grotesque sides of beef and decapitated chickens hanging from their feet, flower shops with rows of brightly colored blooms, hat shops, tea shops, bakeries, and delis lined the labyrinthine halls that made up the Covered Market. It was the end of their day, and most of the shop owners were closing up, but Meriwether resolved to come back some morning soon and do some serious shopping.

"I'll buy you a gelato if you promise not to tell Gran," teased Daniel, only half jokingly.

"What's gelato?" asked Meriwether.

"Italian ice cream," answered Daniel. "It's excellent!"

"Sounds great!" The scone was long gone, and it was still an hour till dinner.

Daniel bought the gelatos, a mix between traditional ice cream and a really thick fruit slushie. "I think we'd better head back now. Gran will have a fit if we're late."

"Okay," answered Meriwether, wondering if she were about to meet her father at last, or if she would once again be put off.

The bus ride was uneventful except for the fact that they had to stand in the aisle because all of the seats were full. Meriwether was not used to the sensation and had some trouble keeping her footing during the inevitable lurches. A little way before their stop, Daniel pulled a cable that ran along the length of the bus. They exited along with an old Indian woman who carried a fishnet shopping bag emitting strange and exotic smells and crossed the street to 240. The old woman traveled along Abingdon then turned down a side street and disappeared. As they approached the house, Meriwether saw a man sitting on a front stoop. From their distance, Meriwether could not be sure if it was number 240 or not, but then Daniel nudged her arm with his elbow and said, "It's your dad outside to meet you."

Meriwether's heart caught in her throat and she fought the impulse to either run into her father's arms or turn around and run the other way. Daniel held back slightly as Meriwether continued forward. As she approached, her father stood slowly. He was tall, although not as tall as he had seemed to Meriwether's five year old self, and thin, but muscular. One strong, well-tanned forearm gripped the iron banister, while his free hand ran itself through a dark head of hair that was beginning to gray above the ears and at the temples. His crinkly eyes looked tired, a bit nervous, and, just like Meriwether remembered, a little sad. He held out his hand and long, sinewy fingers closed around Meriwether's small ones.

"Hello, Meriwether," he said seriously. His voice was deep and kind. His gray-blue eyes searched her hazel ones.

Meriwether knew in that instant that she liked her father. She was so relieved that, despite his reserve, she smiled brightly and felt her face flush. "Hello, Dad."

"I'm very sorry about today. I hope you weren't too disappointed. I trust Daniel here took good care of you?" Dr. Knight's slow bass voice resonated into the evening air.

45

"Oh, yes. Everything was fine," Meriwether willed Daniel to keep silent about the backpack. "Did you finish your project?"

"Only just. I had a deadline moved up on me last minute; a very important exhibit piece. Never wanted to miss your arrival..." Meriwether was struck again with just how tired her father looked. The thought occurred to her that he had probably been up all night completing the restoration.

A wave of maternal instinct prompted Meriwether to take her father by the arm and direct him into the house, "Let's see what Mrs. Doone has waiting for us. I'm starved!"

Daniel, a smile playing across his lips, stuffed his hands in his pockets and whistled into the gathering dusk as he walked back toward City Center and the humble flat he shared with his mother.

Chapter Seven

Traffic was heavy far into the night on Abingdon Road and if Meriwether had not been so exhausted, she might have had trouble falling asleep. As it was, she slept like a baby. She woke up the next morning to a gray and drizzly day, but she didn't mind. She could do with a bit of rest after all the excitement of yesterday, and she decided to spend her day, if the weather kept up, wrapped in a blanket with a book from her father's study.

She dressed in a pair of soft green sweat pants, a clean T-shirt, and magenta low-topped Converse sneakers. She pulled her very wavy (because of the rain) hair into a characteristic pony-tail, brushed her teeth, and splashed cold water on her face. No one had woken her up but she could smell coffee brewing and sausage frying from the kitchen.

She had not given the key to her father last night. Of course, she had every intention of giving it to him at some point, but she had made the conscious decision to wait until she got to know him a little better. Meriwether did not understand the significance of the key, but she did know that it was important. She would wait to reveal the secret she carried until the time was right.

She skipped down the steps, the key knocking gently

against her stomach with each bounce. Mrs. Doone was rolling sausages at the stove and her father was sitting at the table with a cup of coffee, reading the *London Times*.

"Well, and I wasn't expecting to see you this time o' mornin'!" exclaimed Mrs. Doone. "Thought you'd be havin' a bit of a lie in, I did."

"I just woke up," shrugged Meriwether with a grin.

"Good morning, Meriwether," said Dr. Knight, looking up from his paper.

"Morning, dad," returned Meriwether, sitting down next to him with a glass of orange juice Mrs. Doone had just handed her. "Will it rain all day?" asked Meriwether, but her father had already returned his attention to the paper and did not hear the question.

"Most of the mornin', I expect," replied Mrs. Doone. "What will you do with yourself, then?"

"Nothing, actually," responded Meriwether. "Just curl up with a good book, if Dad has one I can borrow."

"That's not nothing," Mrs. Doone took exception. "I wish my Daniel liked to read, might help his studies, if you know what I mean ...But then again, you are your father's daughter," she added with a smile, indicating Dr. Knight, hidden away behind his newspaper, with a nod of her head.

"Seems to me that Daniel's more a..." Meriwether searched for the right words, 'a man of action'. He'd rather be doing than thinking about doing."

"You've summed him up, you have," smiled Mrs. Doone, apparently pleased with this description of her grandson. "Just like his granddad, God love 'im."

"You're husband?" asked Meriwether.

"Aye, me own dear Robert. Dead these fourteen years," Mrs. Doone wiped at a lone tear escaping down her cheek.

"I'm sorry. I didn't mean..." Meriwether wished she could keep her foot out of her mouth.

"Oh, don't mind me. I'm just an old woman," Mrs. Doone took a deep breath. "The Lord giveth, and the Lord taketh away. The day after my Robert died, wee Daniel was born. When Daniel was two, Irene, Daniel's mum, and meself decided to come here to find work, and I soon met a *loovely* young couple looking for a housekeeper. Had a baby coming, you see." Mrs. Doone set a large plate of sausages and poached eggs in front of Meriwether.

"My parents?" asked Meriwether, as hungry for information about her parents as she was for the delicious smelling breakfast.

"Aye, your parents," smiled Mrs. Doone.

Meriwether took a bite of her eggs and tried to think what to ask next. There were so many things she wanted to know, and, obviously, Mrs. Doone was the one to ask. At that moment, however, Mr. Knight folded his morning paper and carefully placed it down on the table in front of him, a curious expression clouding his face.

"What is it, Dad?" asked Meriwether.

"It's happened again," responded Dr. Knight, cryptically.

"What's happened?" Meriwether prodded.

"Another robbery," he answered slowly. Then gaining momentum, "There's been a rash of robberies throughout London, even here in Oxford," at this he exchanged a dark look with Mrs. Doone. "Silver, jewelry, for the most part, electronics . . . all left untouched. Seems the thieves are only after specific items. Items of significance to ...antiquity. Complete collections have been stolen, or sometimes an individual object."

"What was taken this time?" wondered Mrs. Doone.

"A modest collection of samurai swords dating back over a thousand years. They belonged to a Lord Carlisle, and had been passed down in his family for seven generations."

"That's horrible!" Mrs. Doone exclaimed.

"Do the police have any leads?" asked Meriwether.

"None at all, according to the article." Dr. Knight stood up to refill his coffee, "None at all."

"When they find 'em they should string 'em up by their thumbs!" cried Mrs. Doone.

"If they find them," cautioned Dr. Knight, rubbing the back of his neck. "Meriwether, I have some work to do on an article I'm writing. If my clicking away on the computer won't disturb you, your page turning won't bother me. I think I have a few things you might enjoy reading."

"Yeah, sounds great!" So he had been listening to their conversation after all. "Thank you, Mrs. Doone. Breakfast was awesome!"

"Awesome, she says!" Mrs. Doone tinkled with laughter. "Oh dear, and how will I top that?"

Chapter Eight

Hardly a day went by that Daniel did not stop by to visit his grandmother and Meriwether or help out around the house. He mowed and watered the lawn. He helped Dr. Knight repair a leaky faucet. He delivered produce and fresh meat from the market. Usually when he came, he and Meriwether would take their now customary walk through Christ Church Meadow, and then Daniel would show her some new landmark within the city. So far, she had seen the Botanic Garden, the Radcliffe Camera, and the inside of Christ Church Cathedral. They had climbed the 74 feet to the top of Carfax Tower and taken pictures of each other with the city as their backdrop.

Up next, they had planned a tour of the Ashmolean, which Meriwether hoped her father would conduct, and a visit to world-famous Blackwell's Books. Meriwether had become an expert at riding the bus and the sight of cars traveling down the wrong side of the road was, if not normal - less strange now.

For Saturday, Meriwether had thought about going back for another look around the Covered Market. Her plans changed, however, with a gentle rap on her bedroom door.

She put down the letter she had been writing to

Holly. "Come in!"

"Still awake?" Her father peered around the door, and then, reassured she was decent, entered the room. He noticed the fluttering curtains and stepped across the room to close and lock Meriwether's window. "Are you hot?"

"No, I just like the feel of the breeze. I close it when I go to bed . . . too much traffic noise," replied Meriwether.

He looked as if he were about to say one thing, then changed his mind and said another, "How would you like to go to London tomorrow?"

"With you?"

"Yes, with me," her father answered. "I've just received a call from a colleague of mine at the British Museum. He has some pieces he wants me to take a look at. Thought you might like to tag along, but if you and Daniel have other plans . . . ."

"No, that'd be great!" exclaimed Meriwether. "I'd love to!"

"Good. See you tomorrow then, bright and early," said Meriwether's father, taking her hand. "Good Night."

"G'night, Dad."

Dr. Knight softly closed Meriwether's door and she heard him pad, not to his own bedroom, but up to his studio on the third floor. Meriwether had learned a lot in the past week, but her father was still a mystery. He was a studious, driven man who had his finger in many pies. This left little time for chit-chat. They had developed a quiet, comfortable way of spending time together, but Meriwether wanted much more. She clutched the key through her nightshirt, finished the letter to Holly, and turned off the bedside lamp.

Tomorrow's trip to London would be the perfect

opportunity for Meriwether to get to know her dad better. It might even prove the right time to give him Grandmother's key.

Another knock on her door the next morning told Meriwether it was time to get up. She unlocked the window, cracked the pane to let in some fresh air, and dressed in a knee-length gypsy skirt, tank-top, Converse sneakers, and her faithful denim jacket. Her father was waiting for her in the kitchen, minus the good morning smells. Saturday was Mrs. Doone's day off.

"We'll grab something on the way," her dad smiled as a particularly loud rumble escaped Meriwether's belly.

They caught the bus to just shy of City Center, made a quick pit-stop at a hole-in-the-wall deli, and walked on to the bus station armed with goodies and a grande, steaming cup of coffee for Dr. Knight; a not so grande hazelnut steamer for his daughter.

"What will Mrs. Doone do with her day off?" asked Meriwether, happily munching a pastry.

"I believe she has a church fund raiser today," answered her father. "She's been baking and freezing for a month. She'll probably bring in 500 P all by herself!"

"Oh," replied Meriwether glumly," I thought she might be having a real day off. You know, stay in bed all day . . . read a good book . . . veg out in front of the TV. She deserves that."

"Deserves it, yes," said Dr. Knight. "But I don't think she would enjoy it. In the twelve, almost thirteen years that I've known her, the only time I've ever seen her 'put her feet up' was when she had the flu," he chuckled. "And even then, I had to threaten to fire her if she didn't take it easy!"

"Well, I'm glad you didn't have to fire Mrs. Doone," laughed Meriwether. "I don't know what you'd do without her!"

"Neither do I," replied Dr. Knight, soberly. "Neither do I."

The pair reached the bus station and purchased their tickets for London, then sat down on a rubberized bench to wait. Despite the early hour, the station was bustling with activity. "Where does Mrs. Doone go to church?" asked Meriwether, still sipping her steamer.

"St. Mary's in Iffley Village," replied Dr. Knight. "Very interesting architecture . . . early 12th century Roman . . . ." he became lost in his own thoughts for a moment, and then surprised Meriwether by changing the subject completely. "What's Daniel up to today?"

"Oh! He promised his mom he'd help her do some stuff around the house. I think they were going to paint the guest room or something."

"Have you met Daniel's mom yet?" asked Dr. Knight.

"No, not yet," replied Meriwether. "We keep meaning to stop by her office, but we always end up doing something else." A slow smile began to creep across her father's face. "What is it?" Meriwether wondered.

Dr. Knight shook his whole head as if trying to joggle the grin from his face, "Nothing." No luck. "It's nothing . . . just wait . . . ." The smile was catching, and the two shared a good laugh, even though Meriwether had no idea what they were laughing about.

The bus ride to London was spent in easy conversation. Meriwether told her father about Holly and about her stay with the Hart family. Dr. Knight told Meriwether about working with the Ashmolean and other museums. He told her about some of the archaeological digs he had been a part of, and Meriwether realized that those strange and unusual gifts she had received through the years had been procured from all over the globe. This gave her a good, warm feeling inside - to know that wherever her father might have been, in some way he had been thinking of her.

They carefully avoided subjects that were too personal. Grandmother was not mentioned, nor was Meriwether's mother; but by the time they reached Victoria Station, Meriwether knew a whole lot more about her dad than she had before leaving Oxford a mere hour ago.

"We'll go to the museum first, and then have some lunch," explained Meriwether's father. "After that, we'll do some sight-seeing, if you want."

"Yeah, that sounds great!" responded Meriwether eagerly.

The two went down into the bowels of Victoria Station, and Meriwether took her first ride on the Underground. She paid very close attention to everything and decided that it wasn't too complicated. At least everything was in English. The routes were color coded and the stops were clearly marked. All you had to do was know where it was you wanted to go and figure out which line would take you there. Everyone was very polite and a feeling of safety and goodwill pervaded . . . not at all what Meriwether had expected from a subway.

In no time they were exiting the Underground and mounting the stairs up to street level. Meriwether's pace quickened as she glimpsed the great white edifice of the British Museum. She flew up the steps and waited impatiently for her father.

"Excited?" asked Dr. Knight, eyes twinkling with amusement.

"Yes, I can't believe I'm here!" answered Meriwether breathlessly. "I want to see everything!"

"This is one of my favorite places in the world," confided Dr. Knight. "Why don't you go on, and I'll catch up after I've seen Dr. Lymon. Just follow the signs. Here's my visitor's pass," he said, taking a badge out of his pants pocket and affixing it to Meriwether's jacket. "There's Dr. Lymon now. See you in a bit."

Meriwether watched as her father walked toward a large desk and shook hands with a small man with thinning gray hair. Dr. Knight indicated Meriwether to his colleague and as they turned to enter a door behind the desk, Meriwether got a good look at Dr. Lymon. It was the gray man from the plane!

"Small world!" marveled Meriwether to herself. Who would think she had been on an airplane with someone who knew her father? Her hand involuntarily sought the key at her stomach, but all thoughts of Dr. Lymon, of, indeed, the 21st century, disappeared from her mind as she entered through the large archway that led to the Egyptian Room.

Meriwether had no idea how long she had been lost in the treasures of the past when she heard her father's deep voice behind her, "Haven't gotten very far."

"I can't believe I'm actually looking at the Rosetta Stone," Meriwether breathed.

"The key that unlocked the language of the hieroglyphs," replied her father. "Pretty awesome, isn't it."

"Totally."

Meriwether Mystery   Emily Beaver

"I'm pleased that you take such an interest," said Dr. Knight, placing his hand on Meriwether's shoulder. "I believe Daniel's right about you."

"What do you mean?" asked Meriwether.

"He says you're not like most girls," replied her father, smiling. "I think it's a compliment."

Embarrassed, Meriwether blurted, "Dr. Lymon was on my plane."

"That's what he said," said Dr. Knight. "I'm surprised he noticed you, actually . . . or that he remembers. He's normally pretty self-absorbed."

Meriwether smiled, thinking that's exactly what Aunt Phil had said about him. "What was he doing in Texas?"

"Studying Native American pictographs," he answered. "It's a big hobby of his. I told him that we had some out on the ranch and he seemed very interested. Probably should have kept my mouth shut."

"Why?"

"Well, it's not really my place to say whether he can go out there or not," replied Dr. Knight.

"I'm sure Grandmother wouldn't mind. I mean, he does work for the British Museum!" exclaimed Meriwether, excited at the prospect.

"Maybe you're right," he answered, "but your grandfather sure wouldn't have liked it . . . strangers on his property . . . if it wasn't an oil man or a cow man, Daddy didn't want him out there."

"I'm sure Grandmother wouldn't mind," Meriwether reiterated, taking her father's arm. "Just ask her."

"Well, we'll see what comes of it, probably nothing," hesitated Dr. Knight. And then, effectively ending the conversation, "Let's go see the mummies!" declared Dr. Knight.

Chapter Nine

After touring the museum, Meriwether and her father made their way to a small pub called The Cat and Owl for a bite of lunch. Because it was a beautiful day, they decided to take their meal out on the patio. Meriwether removed her jacket and, remembering Daniel's advice, laid it across her lap. She pulled her hair back and took a long swig of the lemonade she had ordered, "with ice." Dr. Knight took an equally long swig of his libation and rolled his shirt sleeves up over his elbows.

"So, what did you think?" Dr. Knight asked, crossing his foot over one knee, his arm draped against the back of his chair.

"It was fascinating!" replied Meriwether, her hazel eyes burning bright with excitement. "You're very lucky."

"**Luck** is when preparation meets opportunity," said her father. "Good things happen and bad things happen. You can't control the outcome of every situation, but you can have a plan." Meriwether thought he was finished, but he went on, "I've had a plan since I was fourteen years old. Read a book called, oh, now what was it? Something about a gateway . . . changed my life . . . ."

"*Gateway to the East*, I brought that book with me!" exclaimed Meriwether, "On the plane!"

"Really? Did you read it? Did you enjoy it? I especially recall the parts about Hong Kong and the Gobi Desert.... What a life he led! I decided then and there that I would see the world and live a life of adventure, no matter the cost!" His face had been lit with remembered passion, but at this last bit, a shadow of a frown crossed his face, and he suddenly looked very much like Grandmother.

Here it was. Meriwether wondered if she should tell her father about the stolen backpack. It seemed trivial, but because she had initially concealed the incident, she was now faced with whether to tell the whole truth and nothing but ... or squirm. She decided to squirm. "I ... I didn't get very far, actually," this was embarrassing because the book had obviously had such a huge impact on her father. "I tried to read it on the plane, but I was so excited that I couldn't concentrate.... I haven't really thought about it since then," this was the truth, just not all of it.

"You'll have to show me the book when we get back home," Dr. Knight continued, completely unaware of the moral dilemma facing his daughter. "You took it from the house, I suppose?" Meriwether nodded her assent. "Of course you did ...Yes, I would very much like to see my old friend again."

This was horrible. Meriwether bit her lip and took a deep breath. "I don't have it."

"Did you loan it to Daniel?" replied Dr. Knight. "Effie is always complaining that the boy won't read, but I'll bet he's reading that!"

"Dad," Meriwether looked her father straight on, "I don't have the book anymore -- because it was stolen."

"Stolen!" exclaimed Dr. Knight. "What do you mean?"

Meriwether felt her face flush and, in an effort to escape her father's searching stare, began compulsively arranging her silverware, "Not just the book . . . my whole backpack . . . at the airport, with Daniel." His face fell with disappointment, and Meriwether rushed on, "I'm sorry, Dad! I'm sorry I didn't tell you about my backpack, and I'm sorry about your book."

"Where was Daniel when this happened?" asked Dr. Knight darkly.

"Buying our lunch. It was my fault. I put it down behind my chair and didn't notice it was gone until after we'd finished eating. I just never thought . . . ."

"Of course you didn't." Dr. Knight reached across the table and took Meriwether's hand as she straightened her salad fork, "And I don't blame Daniel either . . . . I blame myself."

Meriwether gazed at her father with a questioning look and he continued, "I should have been there. I'm sorry, Meriwether. Will you forgive me?"

She had not been expecting this and stammered out, "Yes ...of course I will."

"Did you report the theft?"

"No. Daniel said it was as good as gone, and since there was nothing of value in the backpack . . . ," Meriwether faltered, "I mean, nothing of monetary value ...he thought it wasn't worth reporting." Meriwether waited on pins and needles for her father's reply. She didn't want him to be angry with Daniel.

"Yes, I see his point," said Dr. Knight at last. "You did the right thing."

Meriwether Mystery   Emily Beaver

"Are you very disappointed?" ventured Meriwether.

"Me? No, I'm getting used to it," he answered enigmatically. Their food arrived and as they began to eat, Meriwether thought she heard him mumble something like, "It's karma."

When they were finished, the pair leaned back in their chairs, satisfied, and began to plan the rest of their day. They decided to 'do the tourist thing' and take a double decker bus tour of the city's highlights. From there, Meriwether could determine which sites she wanted to get a closer look at this trip. Dr. Knight promised they would come back soon to take in a show and do more sightseeing. It was impossible to see and do all in one day.

Dr. Knight signaled the waitress to let her know they were ready for their bill. Meriwether stood up to tie her jacket around her waist, and a dark, willowy woman approached the railing that separated the restaurant from the sidewalk. She was dressed in a sleeveless shift with a mandarin collar and wore large square-ish sunglasses.

"Peter, is that you?" purred a low voice with distinct eastern accents.

Dr. Knight looked up from the receipt he was examining. "Dr. Zanjani," he said simply.

"It has been a long time," continued the woman, smiling confidently despite the snub.

"It has," replied Dr. Knight curtly.

"And who is this?" The woman lazily turned her attention to Meriwether.

"This is my daughter, Meriwether. Meriwether, this is Dr. Zanjani," Mr. Knight made the cursory introductions.

Dr. Zanjani extended her hand. "Do not be silly . . .

Dr. Zanjani . . . you may call me Samila. You are very lovely."

Meriwether took Dr. Zanjani's hand reluctantly. There was something about this woman that Meriwether did not like. What's more, Meriwether, for the second time in one day, recognized a fellow passenger from the airplane. Dr. Zanjani did not appear to recognize Meriwether, and in all honesty, Meriwether could not be sure the woman had ever noticed her. Still, there was something funny going on. "Thank you. It's nice to meet you ...err, Samila."

Dr. Zanjani continued, "In a different lifetime, we might have been great friends. But now I must go."

"Goodbye, Meriwether." And with a lingering look at Dr. Knight, "Goodbye, Peter." Dr. Zanjani turned her back with a swish of jet black hair; crocodile sling-backs smoothly disappearing into pedestrian traffic.

Dr. Knight fished in his back pocket for his wallet, and Meriwether waited expectantly for him to elaborate. He did not. He wasn't going to tell her anything! Meriwether told herself that it was none of her business, that if he didn't want to talk about it she should just leave it alone . . . but her curiosity eventually won out.

"Who was that?"

"Dr. Zanjani," replied Dr. Knight, poker faced.

"I know that . . . but who *is* she?" Meriwether pressed.

"Dr. Samila Zanjani, professor of antiquities at Cambridge University. Another . . . colleague," explained Dr. Knight unsatisfactorily; but Meriwether could tell that this was all she was getting out of him. He had stubbornly set his jaw, as Meriwether had so often seen her grandmother do. She decided to retreat and pump him for more information later.

"She gave me the creeps," shivered Meriwether.

"Tell me about it."

Chapter Ten

The double decker tour was a great success. Afterwards, Meriwether and her father made closer inspection of the Tower of London, Westminster Abbey, and St. Patrick's Cathedral, another accomplishment of Sir Christopher Wren. Darkness had firmly settled over the city as they grabbed a quick supper at Victoria Station and boarded the bus back to Oxford.

Meriwether had missed her opportunity to come clean at lunch and tell her father about the key. Something had held her back, but she knew she would have to tell him shortly. Her conscience was beginning to eat at her. Besides, she was dead curious. *Soon*, she promised herself.

Dr. Knight turned on his overhead light and began studying a book on royal lineage he had purchased at Westminster Abbey, but the rhythmic jostling of the bus put Meriwether straight to sleep. She woke up in Oxford, her head lolling uncomfortably against her chest, a powerful crick paining her neck. They caught a city bus from the station and rode home in sleepy silence. Meriwether wanted nothing more than to brush her teeth, which felt like they were wearing socks, and crawl into her nice warm bed. She could bathe in the morning and maybe

Meriwether Mystery   Emily Beaver

go with Mrs. Doone to church.

The moon was little more than a sliver as Dr. Knight fumbled in the darkness for his front door key. Strangely, the porch light was unlit, and Mrs. Doone had failed to answer the door.

"Maybe Mrs. Doone is still at the church . . . or having a late supper with Irene and Daniel," suggested Dr. Knight.

"Maybe she fell asleep and forgot to turn on the light," Meriwether proposed.

"Maybe," echoed her father, unconvincingly.

Finally, the key was located and inserted correctly into the door. Dr. Knight flipped on the entryway light. On top of the umbrella stand, along with a few bills and letters to be mailed, laid Mrs. Doone's bag. "Mrs. Doone?" he called softly.

A soft breeze billowed through the house. Meriwether and her father both turned around to check if they had closed the front door behind them. They had.

"I don't like this," said Dr. Knight in a low voice. "Stay behind me."

Meriwether had a bad feeling too. "Please be okay. Please be okay," she repeated over and over in her head as they made their way through the dining room and into the kitchen, turning on lights as they went. The back door from the kitchen was wide open, the screen knocking gently with the night air. Mrs. Doone sat facing the bay window, slumped over the table, a cup of ice cold tea still clutched in her hand.

Dr. Knight reached for her wrist to check for a pulse. Meriwether could hardly bear to look. "Is . . . is she . . . she's not . . . ?" Meriwether asked through the slits in her

Meriwether Mystery Emily Beaver

fingers as her father ran his hand over Mrs. Doone's skull.

"No, there's a pulse," answered Dr. Knight. "She's been knocked out. There's a knot the size of a golf ball on the back of her head."

"That's horrible!" exclaimed Meriwether. "Who would do that to Mrs. Doone?"

Dr. Knight did not respond. Instead, he walked to the phone and dialed an ambulance. Meriwether sat down and patted Mrs. Doone's arm. "Mrs. Doone, can you hear me? Mrs. Doone, please wake up."

Mrs. Doone's eyelids began to flutter. Her hand jerked, spilling cold tea down her arm and onto the table. "Wha . . . what's that? Oh dear, and look at the mess I've made." She looked at Meriwether and big tears began to roll down her cheeks.

"She's all right, Dad!" cried Meriwether, laughing

and crying at the same time. "Can you bring us a dish towel?"

Mrs. Doone insisted that she did not need an ambulance; that she was perfectly all right. But as one had already been called, she eventually agreed to go to the hospital and get checked for concussion. Dr. Knight called the Pleasant household to let them know what was going on. Daniel's mom was out on a date, so Daniel left a note and met Meriwether and Dr. Knight at the hospital.

Just as she had predicted, Mrs. Doone was checked out okay by the attending physician and released to go home. The police would be notified by the emergency room, and a constable would stop by tomorrow to take her statement and have a look around. By the time the party of four got back to the house, it was past midnight.

Daniel tried his mom again, but she was still out. Despite the late hour, they were all wide awake. "I'll make us some tea," announced Mrs. Doone as they settled around the oak table.

"You most certainly will not," vetoed Dr. Knight. "I'll make the tea. You sit right there and tell us what happened . . . if you're up to it," he added cautiously.

"I'm up to it," replied Mrs. Doone, steeling herself.

"The auction finished early, around 3:00, and Moira Howard drove me home in her little car. We did very well, by the way, and not a cake left that I baked." At the disappointed look on Daniel's face, she added, "Don't worry, dear. I left one out for tomorrow."

Daniel exhaled a breath of relief and Mrs. Doone continued with her story. "I unlocked the door, came in the house, and locked the door back behind me. Nothing was amiss. I came in the kitchen to make a cup of tea, sat down to drink it, and Wham! .... That's it. That's all I remember." Mrs. Doone looked pertly from face to face, gauging the effect of her account.

"Your assailant must have left through the back door, and in a hurry, because it was wide open," said Dr. Knight.

"Maybe he never hit an old woman over the head before and got scared," said Daniel, clenching his fists.

"It does bring up an interesting point, though," Dr. Knight stood and walked over to examine the back door. "There's no sign of forced entry. Whoever did this either knows how to pick a lock . . . or has a key." Dr. Knight continued, "I'm going with the former because the only three people who have a key are sitting in this kitchen.

"That means we're dealing with a professional, a professional who knew our schedule. Knew we'd all be out of the house today ...or would have been had the church auction not ended early. I think he panicked when Mrs. Doone got home and did what he had to do to get out of the house without being seen."

"But who knew we'd all be gone today?" wondered Meriwether. "Our trip to London was last minute . . . not even Daniel knew we were going."

"That's true," answered Dr. Knight. "Dr. Lymon knew I was coming to London, but he didn't know I'd be bringing you. I phoned Gerry to cancel the work we had planned for today, and I think I might have mentioned that you were coming along, but he didn't know about Mrs. Doone."

"But he does know that Saturdays are her day off," Daniel reminded them.

"Yes ..." considered Dr. Knight, furrowing his brow.

Meriwether Mystery   Emily Beaver

"Yes he does ...Look, I know it's late, and Mrs. Doone, if you need to go to bed, just say so, but I think we should split up and search the house. If we discover what's missing, we'll have a better idea what we're dealing with here."

"I'm all right," affirmed Mrs. Doone. "I'll search the living room and the downstairs. Daniel you go with Meriwether to check her room."

"And I'll rummage through my things upstairs," added Dr. Knight. "We'll meet back in the kitchen in, say, 15 minutes."

The small party dispersed, and Daniel and Meriwether went upstairs to examine her room. She opened her door cautiously, and, at first, everything appeared as she had left it. It was only upon closer inspection that she could tell someone had been through her things.

For instance, Meriwether observed that someone had taken everything out of her desk drawers, one drawer at a time, and then put it all back. Everything was in the right drawer, but in the wrong place. Most people probably wouldn't have noticed, but Meriwether did.

Same in her armoire. Her clothes were hanging awkwardly from hangers, as if someone had gone through all the pockets, and *gulp* her underwear had been rifled through. Nothing was missing, but the thief had definitely been looking for something in her room. Meriwether shared her observations with Daniel who stood looking out her window to the now quiet, but for the roar of the occasional lorry, street below.

"Your window is open," observed Daniel.

"Yeah, I cracked it this morning to let the ...," a

horrible thought occurred to Meriwether. "Do you think that's how he got in?"

"Nah, too obvious. How could a bloke climb up a wall facing the street in broad daylight and not get noticed?" replied Daniel. "But still, I'd be more careful if I were you. Someone seems to want something you've got . . . or thinks you've got. First the backpack, and now this. It's starting to look suspicious."

"I've been thinking the same thing," frowned Meriwether, flopping across her bed. "But I don't have anything." Meriwether felt for the key laying against her stomach, "Nothing that's worth anything, anyway."

Daniel sat down in her desk chair and leaned forward, placing his elbows on his knees and clasping his hands loosely. "Maybe it's worth something, and you just don't know it. Go on, Meriwether. Come clean. What is it you've got?"

Meriwether took the chain from around her neck and handed it to Daniel, "Just this."

"And what is *this*?"

"Grandmother gave it to me the night before I came here. She made me promise to give it to my dad," explained Meriwether as she rolled over on her stomach to face Daniel. "I don't know what it means."

"And why haven't you given it to him?" asked Daniel, examining the key.

"I don't know . . ." answered Meriwether feebly. Daniel raised one eyebrow, appraising her shrewdly. "I guess I just wanted to wait until I knew him a little better..."

"And ..." prompted Daniel.

"And..." Meriwether continued, "I want to know

what's behind it! You don't know my grandmother. She's barely mentioned my dad's name in the last eleven years, and all of a sudden she's packing me off to England and giving me this mysterious key without any explanations. Grandmother is not mysterious. She's the most down to earth person I know. The whole thing is completely out of character! I want to know what's going on, and I was afraid that if I gave Dad the key right off the bat, he'd just take it and not explain anything. I was never not going to give it to him . . . . I was just waiting." By this time, Meriwether was pacing around the room like a mad woman, her eyes blazing with indignation.

Daniel lifted his arm in front of him; palm splayed, and chuckled, "Alright, alright! The prosecution rests . . . witness may step down!"

"Thank you," quipped Meriwether, perching on the end of her bed.

"I'll bet you this is what he's after." said Daniel, dangling the chain in front of him. "This key is very old, ancient I'd say. Who else knows about it?"

Meriwether thought for a moment. "Well, I did meet a nice woman, a farmer's wife from -- what was it? -- Bournton! ...on the plane. She'd been in Dallas visiting her daughter. I, uh, I sort of needed someone to talk to, and she was so friendly ...I told her about the key."

"Did you have it around your neck? Did you show it to her?"

"Yes, I did have it around my neck," Meriwether thought back to their conversation, "but, no, I didn't show it to her."

"Why not?"

"I don't know . . . I just didn't. She must have

assumed that I had it tucked away somewhere in my luggage," Meriwether replied. "But you don't think Mrs. Shockley had anything to do with this, do you? She seemed completely genuine, and I saw Mr. Shockley pick her up at the airport. He looked every bit a farmer."

"It's hard to say," answered Daniel, thinking out loud. "I'm willing to trust your instincts about Mrs. Shockley, but have you thought about who else might have overheard your conversation?"

Bells and whistles started going off in Meriwether's brain. "Oh my gosh, Daniel, I almost forgot! Today, in London, I saw two different people I recognized. Mrs. Shockley and I sat together from Dallas to Chicago. Two other people on that flight were also on my flight to London . . . and I saw them both today!"

Meriwether told Daniel about her father's meeting with Dr. Lymon and the seemingly chance encounter with Dr. Zanjani.

"They were both sitting close enough to hear me talking with Mrs. Shockley, if they were really trying."

"That's really strange," reflected Daniel. "The strangest part about it is that they both know your dad and they're both in his field. I think you'd better show this key to your dad right now, so we can get to the bottom of this."

"You're right," agreed Meriwether glancing at her watch. "Our 15 minutes are up."

They descended the stairs and waited a moment to be joined by Dr. Knight and Mrs. Doone. Mrs. Doone spoke first, "Well, and nothing's missing downstairs that I can tell."

"Nothing in my room or in the studio either," added

Dr. Knight, looking at Meriwether, waiting for her report.

"Nothing's gone," responded Meriwether, sheepishly returning her father's gaze, "but Daniel and I think we might know what he was after."

The surprise of the two adults was evident as Meriwether forged on. She slowly removed the chain from around her neck and handed it to her father.

"The night before I came here, Grandmother gave me this key. She told me to give it you. I'm sorry I didn't give it to you sooner ...I, well, I was hoping you would explain it to me, and I didn't think you would until we got to know each other better."

Dr. Knight clutched the chain in his hand, and, to Meriwether's dismay, sunk his head down into his fists, shaking his head slowly from side to side.

Meriwether looked frightfully from Daniel to Mrs. Doone, but they both shrugged their shoulders. Presently, Dr. Knight collected himself and began in a low, husky voice, "You might as well all hear this, and I can only hope that each of you will be able to forgive me for not being the man you thought me to be.

"Meriwether, you remember the conversation we had just this afternoon — about the book I read as a young man?" Meriwether nodded as her father continued. "Well, from that moment on, I decided that I wanted a different sort of life from the one my parents, especially my father, had planned for me. You see, I was supposed to go to college, get a decent education, then return to the ranch and take over when my father was ready. I believe they both thought it was a passing phase, that I would put 'childish' ideas of adventure behind me and eventually accept my responsibilities at home. But by the time I

Meriwether Mystery   Emily Beaver

turned 18, nothing had changed.

"The afternoon of graduation, in fact, my father and I had a huge argument. It was Daddy's way or the highway. I chose the highway. The day I turned eighteen I had gained control of my trust fund. That same afternoon that we argued, I went to the bank and withdrew the money. The day after graduation, I left home and haven't been back, except for my father's funeral seven years ago."

"I'm sorry Dad, I didn't know."

"Wait, I'm not finished," sighed Dr. Knight studying his hands, the chain entwined in his clasped fingers. "I was young, and impetuous - but that's no excuse. I was very angry with my father for being so hard-nosed, and I was angry with my mother for not taking my part. I wanted to do something that would hurt them as much as they had hurt me . . . . So when I left, I took a very special box that belonged to Mother. It was extremely old and had been passed down through many generations in her family." Dr. Knight's and Mrs. Doone's eyes locked.

"The box contained valuable items that held sentimental value for my parents . . . the pearl necklace Daddy gave Mother as a wedding gift, my father's college ring, a pocket watch that commemorated their first anniversary . . . as well as, I believe, love letters Daddy sent during their courtship. I say 'I believe' because I haven't seen inside the box since childhood. I had watched Mother take it down and open it up enough times throughout the years to know where she kept it and what it held, but the box itself was kept locked. This key that you have given me, Meriwether, is the key that unlocks the box I took from my parents' home almost 25 years ago."

"Why did she send the key with me?" asked

75

Meriwether Mystery — Emily Beaver

Meriwether, blown away by her father's confession.

"I don't know," thought her father. "I'm hoping it means that she's forgiven me. You see, we've never once spoken of it. I had my chance with her when I came home for the funeral, but I was too ashamed to mention it. I missed my chance with my father altogether. He died believing me a good for nothing thief of a son. I'll never be able to forgive myself for that."

Meriwether didn't know what to say. She reached out and grasped her father's hands across the table. "I'm sure it means she's forgiven you. It all makes sense now . . . she seemed so sad. Don't you see, now you can return the box and the key, and everything will be all right again?"

Again, Dr. Knight looked at Mrs. Doone with a pained expression. "I don't have the box anymore."

"You didn't sell it!" cried Meriwether in horror.

"No, I didn't sell it," retorted Dr. Knight. "I never once had any intention of selling it, or its contents . . . and thought a thousand times of packing it up and air mailing it home . . . . Why I didn't . . . . No. I didn't sell it. It was stolen . . . about a year ago, from this very house."

"The thief in the papers who's stealing all the antiques?" asked Meriwether.

"I can't prove it, of course. But, yes, that's what I think."

"Then it's all related!" Meriwether jumped up excitedly and began to pace around the kitchen. "Whoever stole the box has come back for the key! They obviously think something important is inside and don't want to damage the box by picking the lock."

"But you leave out something very important, Meriwether. After the box was stolen, I formulated a list of suspects - people who knew about the box, whom I deemed capable of thievery. The list was very short. How could any of those people have known about the key?"

"That's just it!" exclaimed Meriwether. "I was just telling Daniel that I sort of poured my heart out to a really nice lady on the plane. I noticed several people on the flight, people who were sitting close enough to eavesdrop on our conversation, and I saw two of them today!" she ended dramatically.

Dr. Knight looked confused, "Dr. Lymon ... and ..."

"Dr. Lymon -- and Dr. Zanjani!" cried Meriwether triumphantly.

Dr. Knight stared into his tea cup and thought for a moment. At last, he raised his head and said, "Yes. They both knew about it. I had of late become very interested in the box. As my knowledge of ancient artifacts increased, I began to wonder just how old the box might be. I showed the box to several of my colleagues to get their opinions on it, telling them only that it had been in my mother's family for many generations."

"When it was stolen, the police asked for a list of people who knew the box existed. I gave them the names of the people I had consulted. Each person was questioned, as a matter of course, but they were all eventually ruled out as suspects. I was forced to accept their findings, but I still had my suspicions. Of course, I don't think the authorities were too concerned about a carved wooden box, no matter how old it might have been."

"Did you suspect Dr. Lymon or this Dr. Zanjani?" asked Daniel, speaking up at last.

"I eventually ruled out Lymon. He's a real straight arrow, spends every waking moment at the museum. He has a flat somewhere in London, but half the time he sleeps in his office. I just can't see him taking the trouble - or the risk - to steal something when he is surrounded by so many wonderful things at the museum. Besides, his thing is Native American artifacts; not thirteenth century Anglo-Saxon."

"What about Dr. Zanjani?" prodded Meriwether.

"Dr. Zanjani is a horse of a different color," brooded Dr. Knight. "I wouldn't put much past Samila Zanjani," Mrs. Doone snorted in assent. "Her tastes tend to be very - extravagant . . . more than a university professor can afford at any rate. She was at the top of my suspect list. Especially after . . . ."

"Especially after what?" urged Meriwether, determined to get the whole story.

"Especially after your father sent her packing, that's what!" chirped Mrs. Doone. "I never liked that woman, not for a second. Dr. Knight was taken in for a bit, but he caught on to her soon enough."

"So you and Dr. Zanjani were . . . ." Meriwether couldn't quite bring herself to finish the rest of the sentence. Bile had begun to rise up into the back of her throat.

"Yes," her father answered squarely. "For a bit. Let's just say . . . she can be very charming . . . and I suppose I was lonely."

Meriwether and Mrs. Doone both harrumphed and crossed their arms across their chests. "So how come I never met her?" wondered Daniel.

"Well, as I say, the - uh - *relationship* did not last long. She was only here at the house a few times. I suppose you just missed her."

"Too bad," smiled Daniel. "She sounds like a fox."

Dr. Knight smiled in spite of himself, and Mrs. Doone and Meriwether both rolled their eyes and pulled in their arms more tightly. Dr. Knight cleared his throat and guided the conversation back to the topic at hand. "I do not believe our encounter with Dr. Zanjani today had anything to do with chance."

"Neither do I, but how did she know we would be there?" questioned Meriwether.

"The Cat and Owl is one of my favorite lunch spots in London, and Samila knows it. I believe the meeting was designed to throw suspicion away from her - give her an alibi, so to speak. But her appearance makes me suspect her all the more, and it confirms something I'd wondered about before. She must have an accomplice."

"I saw her with a man at Gatwick," recalled Meriwether.

"What do you remember about him?" asked her father.

"Lots of white hair. Blue eyes," Meriwether thought back, "not very tall - they were about the same height.

". . . . Very fashionable. Very handsome," she blushed slightly at Daniel's surprised look. "Does it sound like anyone you know?"

"No, but it sounds typical. He's probably just her latest catch. I think there's someone else; someone who tipped her off about today; someone who's doing her dirty work."

At the same time, Daniel and Dr. Knight both growled, "Gerry."

"Will you tell all this to the police tomorrow?" demanded Meriwether, afraid of what her father might take it upon himself to do.

"I don't think so," answered Dr. Knight, coolly. "I think I'll have a little talk with my assistant, man to man."

"I don't think that's a very good idea!" cried Meriwether. "What if he does something crazy?"

"And I'm agreeing with Meriwether, Dr. Knight. You must be careful. No telling what the boy might do if he's backed into a corner!" added an anxious Mrs. Doone.

Daniel stuck out his chest, "I want to go with you!"

"No, no," said Dr. Knight calmly. "I think this is something I can handle by myself. You're forgetting; the man is a coward. I know what its like - to be a coward. But I refuse to be one any longer. Gerry's going to tell me what he and Samila have done with Mother's box. I'm going to get it back. I'm going to make things right."

Chapter Eleven

Meriwether drug herself out of bed early the next morning. Her arms and legs felt like they were made of lead, but she was sure that Mrs. Doone would be going to church, and she didn't want her to go alone. Yawning violently, she pulled a sweatshirt on over her pajamas and padded down the stairs in stocking feet. Sure enough, there was Mrs. Doone in her house coat, cooking herself a breakfast of bacon and eggs - hair and makeup already done.

"Meriwether! What are you doing up?" exclaimed Mrs. Doone. "Do you want some breakfast? It won't take me a minute to whip up a bit more."

"No thanks. I'll just eat a bowl of cereal. I can do it," responded Meriwether, pulling the box from the cabinet. "I just wanted you to know that I'm going to church with you this morning . . . and not to leave without me. How's your head?"

"A little tender . . . couldn't sleep on my back," answered Mrs. Doone, gingerly feeling the knot with her fingertips. "I'm so glad you'll be coming with me. St. Mary's is l*oo*vely!"

"Does Daniel or his mom ever go with you?" asked Meriwether.

"Daniel does sometimes, but he usually goes with his mother to St. Aldate's. It's a little more modern . . . lots of young people. You should go with them sometime, but I'm so glad you'll be with me today. A bit o' company will be nice."

"Does Dad ever go . . . to church, I mean?" wondered Meriwether.

Mrs. Doone shook her head slowly, "Not for a long time, dear. Not for a long time."

Meriwether smoothed her hair into a low pony-tail and dressed in a simple a-line skirt, matching summer weight sweater, and black ballet flats. It felt strange to no longer have the key hanging around her neck, but Meriwether didn't own any jewelry - other than her glow-in-the-dark wrist watch, so she had nothing to replace the empty sensation with. She met Mrs. Doone, dressed in a smart mauve-ish pink skirt suit and fluid striped shirt that tied at the throat, in the entry-way at the foot of the stairs.

Mrs. Doone tied a silk scarf, kerchief style, about her head, grabbed her Sunday purse, which had replaced her bulky everyday bag, and the two left the house. They crossed the street and followed the practice fields away from City Center. Veering steadily left, they made their way further into the countryside. They came to a stream and followed it, eventually crossing over a small bridge, not unlike the one Meriwether and Daniel frequented on their walks through the meadow.

Meriwether could not think of a nicer way to arrive at church. She thought of all the Sunday mornings at home, rushing to get ready, making sure she looked just right. Then she thought of the few times she had spent the night with Holly on a Saturday night. Talk about chaos!

Usually, by the time everyone actually got in the car (to travel a far shorter distance than Meriwether and Mrs. Doone had just traversed) Mrs. Hart was yelling, Holly and her brothers were arguing, and Mr. Hart was gripping the steering wheel, white knuckled with impatience and irritation.

How much better, to walk along in silent meditation, enjoying the world that God created. Meriwether drank in her surroundings, happy to be alive and, despite the events of the last twenty-four hours, or maybe because of them, thankful for her many blessings.

Across the bridge, the footpath developed into a road which led the pair into a little village lined with yellow stone houses and friendly fences covered with profusions of climbing roses. They turned right on Church Way ending in a cul-de-sac in front of the muted stone facade of St. Mary's.

"We'll enter at the West Door," said Mrs. Doone, guiding Meriwether around to the front of the church. A cut stone walkway led up to enormous wooden doors, which opened into the baptistry. The doors were flanked by a series of arched carvings of what looked to Meriwether like gigantic teeth. Two rows of birds' heads and beaks lay outside of the "teeth", and crowning it all, in a semi-circular arch, were carved various symbols that Meriwether could not quite make out.

"Good morning, Effie," greeted a tall young man with thick blonde hair and a mustache. They shook hands as he handed her a program for the day's service.

"Good morning, Spence," returned Mrs. Doone. "I'd like you to meet Meriwether Knight, Dr. Knight's daughter. She's visiting for the summer."

Meriwether Mystery   Emily Beaver

"Hello, Meriwether," said Spence, shaking Meriwether's hand. "We're very glad to have you this morning."

"Thank you," replied Meriwether as she was also handed a program.

Crossing the threshold into the church building, Meriwether had the strange sensation that she was entering the mouth of a giant beast. "What do those carvings mean?" she wondered aloud as they made their way to Mrs. Doone's usual spot.

"No one knows for sure," answered Mrs. Doone. "The church was built in the Roman style in the early 12th century. People were very superstitious back then. I've heard it explained that the triangular carvings were meant to represent the teeth of a dragon, whose purpose was to keep evil spirits from entering the sanctuary."

"Kind of like a gargoyle?"

"Exactly."

Meriwether looked back toward the entrance and noticed a large, circular stained glass window set atop the doors. Sunlight was streaming through the glass, illuminating the design and dappling the church with parti-colored light. Mrs. Doone followed Meriwether's gaze. She leaned over as the service began, whispering, "The Eye of God."

Meriwether enjoyed the high church atmosphere of the Anglican service - so different from what she was used to at home. At the end of the service, the minister, dressed in robes of black, shook hands with Mrs. Doone and Meriwether. Meriwether was invited to come back next week as the congregation migrated out of the church and onto the green. She was introduced to many of Mrs. Doone's fellow parishioners, where talk consisted mainly of the church auction and its success.

Mrs. Doone never said a word about last night. Meriwether hadn't expected that she would, but she wondered if Mrs. Doone would confide in some of her closer friends, like Moira Howard, about the incident. Mrs. Howard offered the two a ride home but they politely refused, choosing instead to quietly make their way home in the same manner they had come.

By the time they got home, Meriwether was starving. The delicious aroma of pot roast met them as they entered the house, and Meriwether could hear the sounds of people laughing in the kitchen. Dr. Knight, Daniel, and what had to be Daniel's mother, Irene, were sitting at the kitchen table. As Meriwether and Mrs. Doone entered the kitchen, Irene jumped up and began to fuss over her mother.

Meriwether tried not to stare, but it was very difficult because Irene Pleasant was about as different from Mrs. Doone as a person could get. She was a big woman, not fat - but tall and strong. She had a head full of frizzy (their only likeness) shocking red hair that was pulled back from her face with a violently clashing violet sash. She wore a long, flowing floral dress that buttoned all the way up the front, a lilac, open-weave cardigan, and platform heeled strappy black sandals. Her fingernails and toenails were painted a deep shade of burgundy, and there was a little tattoo of a heart, pierced by an arrow, on her ankle.

Meriwether, intent on avoiding her dad's eyes, looked at Daniel instead with what she hoped was a blank expression. Daniel grinned and shrugged as if to say, "That's me mum!"

Mrs. Doone shooed her daughter's attentions away as she laced an apron on over her Sunday suit and took the roast from the oven. Irene Pleasant seemed to notice Meriwether for the first time. "And you must be

Meriwether! Pretty as a picture! Daniel talks about you all the time!" She said all this while holding firmly to both of Meriwether's shoulders and turning her this way and that, appraising her from all angles.

"Yes, ma'am," answered Meriwether breathlessly, still clutched in Irene's grasp. "It's very nice to finally meet you, Ms. Pleasant."

"Oh, posh!" exclaimed Irene, releasing Meriwether suddenly. "None of this 'ma'am' and 'Ms. Pleasant' business with me! You'll make me feel old, you will! Irene will do."

"Yes, ma' …uh, Irene. Thanks," answered Meriwether, trying to collect herself.

"Let's help Mum and set the table," nudged Irene chummily, taking the good dishes from a free-standing cabinet. Meriwether removed some silverware from the drawer and followed Irene into the dining room. "You can tell me all about America," chatted Irene. "Did you know that when I was a little girl, I dreamed of living on a cattle ranch?"

Talk at dinner carefully avoided the topic that was foremost in all of their minds. It was not until they were all using the bottoms of their forks to pick up the last crumbs of Mrs. Doone's exceptional coconut pound cake that Irene leaned in conspiratorially, "Alright, enough's enough. Spill it."

"What do you mean? Didn't Daniel tell you what happened?" answered Dr. Knight in confusion.

"He told me a bit, but I want the whole story," replied Irene, looking from face to face around the table. "And I want in on the action."

"The action?" echoed Dr. Knight.

"The take-down. No one clonks me mum over the head and gets away with it!"

Meriwether dug her fingernail into her thumb and tried not to smile. It sounded like Irene had watched one too many detective shows on the telly. Still, she understood how Irene felt. Meriwether opened her mouth to speak, but closed it up again, wincing from the pain of a kicked shin. Daniel was staring at her from across the table - the message unmistakable . . ., *don't say anything*.

"I told you Mum," began Daniel, "There was an intruder, and he knocked Gran out when she got home too early. Nothing was taken, but Dr. Knight thinks he might know who it was. He'll take care of it."

"What about the police?" shot Irene.

"The police have been informed and given the facts of the situation," returned Dr. Knight. "Two officers came by while you were at church," he explained to Mrs. Doone. "They had a look around, asked some questions, dusted for fingerprints here and there; said they'd be back tomorrow to take your statement."

"And what of your suspicions?" wondered Irene.

"They are only that. Suspicions," answered Dr. Knight. "It's true. I think I know who might have had a hand in it . . . but the last thing I want to do is have him scared off by the police before I get a chance to talk to him myself."

Irene leaned back in her chair, crossing her arms across her chest. "Like I said, I want in."

"I appreciate the offer, Irene . . . and I promise to keep you informed, but this is something I need to do myself."

Irene, with her eyes opened just a slit, pursed her

lips and gnawed on the inside of her cheek, and with burgundy fingernails tapping said, "Fine. Just take care of it."

"I will. I promise."

After lunch, Daniel and Meriwether offered to do the dishes while Mrs. Doone, who was looking a bit done in, went to lie down for a nap. Daniel's mom took the bus home, and Dr. Knight disappeared into his studio. Speaking in low voices, the two rehashed the events of and leading up to yesterday's break in.

"Where do you think he's got the key?" asked Meriwether.

"Dunno...Somewhere safe I hope," answered Daniel, handing Meriwether a plate.

Wash. Rinse. Dry.

Wash. Rinse. Dry.

"What about your mom?" wondered Meriwether. "What's up with that?"

"Ah, Mum's alright," said Daniel. "Got a big mouth is all...Can't seem to help herself, really. It's just best not to give her all the details . . . not if you want it kept quiet, anyhow."

Wash. Rinse. Dry.

Wash. Rinse. Dry.

"I haven't met Gerry. What's he like?"

"Young. Dark hair. Dark eyes. Bad teeth."

"Is that all?"

"I don't like 'im."

"Why not? . . . I mean, I know why not . . . but do you just not like him now, or did you never not like him?" Meriwether wasn't sure she had said what she meant to say, but Daniel seemed to understand.

"Never liked him," he confirmed.

"Why not?"

"Dunno . . ." Daniel thought for a moment. "I just don't trust him. He's always real polite to your dad or me Gran or whoever - but I get the feeling that he doesn't really mean it. Like on the inside he's rolling his eyes and thinking everybody's a joke. Does that make any sense?"

"Yeah, I know what you mean. I hate that," agreed Meriwether.

"Yeah. Anyway, here's the thing . . . I don't think your dad should go off to talk to him alone."

"You think Gerry might do something?" Meriwether could feel the little hairs at the back of her neck prickle.

"I think it's possible."

"But he'll never let us go with him! You heard him. This is something he wants to do alone . . . like a point of honor or something," gushed Meriwether, becoming genuinely afraid for her father.

Daniel looked around, making sure they were alone. "He doesn't have to know. And there is no 'us' in this. Too dangerous. I'm gonna tail 'im . . . just to make sure nothing goes wrong."

"But what could *you* do if something did?" asked Meriwether fearfully.

"Go get help. Tackle Gerry from behind. Whatever needed to be done." Daniel's full concentration was devoted to the large platter he was carefully soaping. He would not look Meriwether in the eye, but she could sense his determination - could even feel it somehow. She decided not to argue, but resolved just as stubbornly to make sure that if Daniel were there to help her dad, she would be there to help Daniel.

Chapter Twelve

Meriwether decided that the best way to keep tabs on Daniel was to stick to her father. She dressed before going down to breakfast the next morning, prepared to follow him from a distance whenever he chose to leave the house.

After an uncomfortable breakfast -- Dr. Knight had become more distracted than ever, responding to Meriwether's attempts at conversation with grunts and blank stares -- Meriwether positioned herself in the study, pretending to read a book, but actually listening for and watching her father's movements. From this vantage point, she would know if he received a phone call or left the house.

At 11:00, she heard the sound of heavy shoes clomping down the stairs. The front door opened and closed, and Meriwether peeked from behind the curtains out the front picture window as her father strode purposefully up Abingdon Rd., toward City Center. After he was a pretty good way down the street, Meriwether saw Daniel emerge from his stake-out point, across the street behind a large tree, to follow Dr. Knight.

Meriwether watched Daniel for a full minute, and then called out to Mrs. Doone, "I'm going for a walk! Be back in a while!"

"But what about your lunch, dear?" Mrs. Doone poked her head out of the kitchen.

"I'm not hungry," Meriwether fibbed, her stomach grumbling. "I'll eat something when I get back."

"Suit yourself!" And then in a different tone, "Do be careful."

"Sure thing!" Meriwether answered with more confidence than she felt. "You too."

Meriwether let herself out the door and quickly skipped down the front steps. She would have to hurry not to lose Daniel. She heard the sound of the door deadbolting behind her and assured herself that Mrs. Doone would be safe in the house alone.

Sticking to the opposite side of the street from Daniel, Meriwether could keep him in her line of sight without setting off his radar. Besides, he was so busy following Dr. Knight that he didn't even think about someone following him. This thought gave Meriwether a sudden uneasy feeling because, before that, she had forgotten to wonder if someone might be following her.

She stopped abruptly, looking suspiciously down both sides of the street. She didn't know who she thought it could be . . . Mrs. Doone? . . . Irene? . . . gulp, Gerry? She didn't see anyone she recognized or anyone fitting the description Daniel had given her of Gerry. Satisfied, she resumed her tracking of Daniel, who was even further ahead of her than before.

She quickened her step, but even though her legs had become accustomed to walking, the pace Daniel was keeping in an attempt to stay up with Dr. Knight was giving her a stitch in the side. She knew she would lose him if she stopped to catch her breath, so she pushed on, rubbing her aching side as she walked.

On past City Center they went. Meriwether hung back as Daniel crossed the street and approached the Ashmolean, entering the building from an employee entrance at street level. A few moments later, afraid to let Daniel get too far ahead, Meriwether followed him in.

He had disappeared. Meriwether was standing in a long, deserted hallway - silent but for the gentle hum of overhead fluorescent lighting. The dingy hallway was lined with unmarked doors. Meriwether could think of nothing else to do but start listening at doorways to try to find the right room.

She tip-toed down the passage, pressing her ear at each door, straining to hear through the metal, terrified that someone might come down the hallway at any moment and catch her snooping. *I'll just tell them I'm looking for my father's office. That wouldn't be a lie . . . exactly.*

At last, she came to a door toward the end of the hallway and thought she could hear the low rumble of male voices on the other side. The voices, however, sounded very far away. Meriwether couldn't think what good she was doing standing in the hall with her ear to the door, just waiting for someone to happen along and ask her what in the world she thought she was doing, so she decided to carefully try the doorknob. It turned easily in her hand, and Meriwether quietly let herself into a dark room lined with shelf after shelf of goodness knows what - it was too dark to see properly.

The voices were louder now that she was inside the door, but she still could not make out what they were saying. Meriwether crept along the narrow aisle between the shelving, toward a small patch of light at the end of the corridor, until she came to another door, partially ajar. The voices were coming from the other side of that door. She leaned in more closely when, suddenly, someone came from behind, reaching around the front of her waist with one arm, the other hand clamping tightly across her mouth.

"Shhh!" whispered the assailant in her ear. Meriwether's eyes were wide, and if she had thought for a moment, she would have realized who it was, but she wasn't thinking, she was reacting. She stomped a foot, but instead of being released, she was only gripped more tightly.

"That was my foot, you idiot!" hissed a familiar voice in her ear. She realized at once whose voice it was, but the knowledge did nothing to calm her down.

"You scared me half to death!" she hissed back.

"What are you doing here?" Daniel pulled her back into a small cubby separating where the shelving ended and the door began.

Meriwether could feel her face flushing, and she was glad that the darkness was hiding her. "I'm following you, if you must know!"

"Worried about me?" She could hear the grin in his voice.

"I just wanted in on the *take down*," Meriwether started snickering toward the end of this and they both had to really fight not to make any noise - nervous laughter threatening to get the better of them.

"Shhh! Listen." Daniel clutched Meriwether's arm. "They're getting into it now."

Meriwether Mystery Emily Beaver

Sure enough, their voices were raised. Meriwether could hear her father saying, "Tell me what you know, Gerry, and maybe the police will cut you a deal." She wasn't at all sure that her father had any basis for saying that, and apparently Gerry wasn't buying it either because, next thing you know, there was a giant CRASH!!! and Gerry came bolting through the door that Meriwether and Daniel were hiding behind.

Meriwether didn't have time to think, other than the realization that it was her father who got crashed and not Gerry. All she had time to do, and it turned out to be more effective than anything she might have done had she been given all day to come up with a plan, was stick her foot out from behind the door into Gerry's path. He went tumbling and knocked head first into a row of shelves - some very heavy objects raining down on top of him. Next thing you know, Daniel had him straddled, but that was really not necessary because Gerry was down for the count.

"I've got Gerry! You go check on your dad!"

Meriwether hurried into the lighted room, a workroom of sorts, kind of like the science labs at school. Dr. Knight was sitting on the green and white speckled linoleum floor, legs splayed, back propped up against one of the lab tables. He was rubbing his head with one hand and holding a shattered piece of pottery in the other.

"Are you okay, Dad?" Meriwether knelt down beside her father, lightly feeling his head for any major injuries.

Dr. Knight groaned as he attempted to sit up further against the table. "I'm all right . . . better than this 5th century urn, at any rate. Help me up, Meriwether."

"Are you sure? Maybe you should stay put for a minute."

"I'm sure. He didn't get away did he?"

"No, we stopped him."

"So much for my one man job. You followed me here I suppose?"

"Well, Daniel followed you, and I followed Daniel ...I hope you're not angry." Meriwether took one of her father's arms and hefted him up. He held on to the side of the work table to steady himself.

"No . . . not angry, I should have known." Dr. Knight tried a smile, but it came out more of a grimace.

After a few moments, when Dr. Knight felt like he could walk, Meriwether helped him out of the work room and back into the storage area where Daniel still had Gerry pinned. Dr. Knight flipped on the light (more fluorescent buzz), and Meriwether saw hundreds of artifacts lining the shelves, each tagged with a short description and an identification number. Two iron statues of some pagan god had fallen on Gerry. The idols appeared unharmed. Meriwether stooped down to pick them up and return them to their places on the shelf. Dr. Knight knelt down next to the prostrate Gerry and slapped him firmly across the face.

Gerry came to, shooting them all a look of pure malevolence. "Give me a name, Gerry. I know you couldn't have planned all of this," demanded Dr. Knight.

Gerry spat on the floor, "I'm not giving you anything."

"Very well, then. Meriwether, go back through the lab and into my office. Call the police. Tell them we have the thief that all of England has been looking for."

Meriwether turned, thinking; *this may take awhile* as she was unused to the foreign telephone system.

She'd only taken a step or two, however, before Gerry yelled, "Stop!"

She turned on her heel, caught her father's eye, and waited. "Look, I did the jobs at your house . . . and I panicked and knocked the old lady . . ." Daniel's arm drew back, his hand tightening into a fist.

"Let him finish, Daniel," cautioned Dr. Knight. Reluctantly, Daniel lowered his arm and relaxed his knuckles; his fingers continued to clench involuntarily in readiness.

"But I didn't have anything to do with those London jobs," Gerry continued, straining his neck as far away from Daniel as possible. "She must have gotten someone else to pull those."

"She?" questioned Dr. Knight expectantly.

"Oh, come off it! You know who I'm talking about!"

"I want to hear it from you."

"Dr. Z, that's who!" spat Gerry, eyes darting nervously. "And I don't mind tellin' you I'm as good as fish food if she finds out it's me who's ratted her out," he ended miserably.

"Black market?"

"I'm not saying anything more. Call the police. Be my guest." Gerry shut his mouth with a snap and refused to say another word.

"What do we do with him?" asked Daniel. "I can pop him in the mouth . . . then he might talk!" he added hopefully.

"Never mind," answered Dr. Knight. "Let him go."

"What!" exclaimed Daniel and Meriwether in unison.

"He's ruined professionally. I'll see to that," replied Dr. Knight. "We have nothing on him except a confession I doubt he will repeat to the police. Let him go, and we have a better chance of catching up to Samila. If she gets wind that her accomplice has been arrested, she'll disappear, and we'll never find Mother's box."

"But what if he goes straight to Dr. Zanjani?" wondered Meriwether. "He'll tip her off and then they'll both get away!"

"I doubt that," responded her father. "I think this is pretty serious business, and if our little friend knows what's good for him he'll steer clear of Zanjani. I don't think she would be very pleased if she knew we were on to him." Dr. Knight stared hard at Gerry. Gerry squirmed under Daniel's weight, itching to get free. He kept looking about wildly as if he expected Dr. Zanjani and her henchmen to sweep in at any moment.

"Let him go, Daniel. That's right." Daniel eased up on Gerry, who scrambled away like the rat he was without a word or a look behind him.

The three watched him go, and then turned toward one another expectantly. The understanding was tacit. . . they were all in this together.

"Now what?" Meriwether wondered.

"Now we go to London," answered her father. "Samila keeps a flat there. It's our best chance of tracking her down."

"But she could be almost anywhere!" exclaimed Daniel. "Don't you think she'll keep trying for the key? Maybe we should just stay here and let her come to us."

"Yes, I do think she'll keep trying for the key," answered Dr. Knight. "In fact, I shudder to think to what lengths she might go to get what she wants. But the fact is that she won't risk doing it herself. If she can't find Gerry, she'll get suspicious - she might even run. We have no time to waste. We must take the offensive and find her before she finds a way to get to us."

They nodded in agreement. Dr. Knight continued, "Now, not a word of this to Mrs. Doone. She would be beside herself with worry. We'll go home and tell her that we scared Gerry off. I'll pretend to have extended business in London and invite the two of you to come with me. We'll send Mrs. Doone to stay with your mom for a few days, Daniel."

"She won't like that," said Daniel behind a grin.

"It can't be helped - only way to make sure she's safe," replied Dr. Knight. "I'll clean up around here and make the necessary arrangements. We leave tomorrow."

Meriwether Mystery Emily Beaver

Chapter Thirteen

So it happened that just three days after her first excursion to London, Meriwether found herself returning - not to sightsee, but to catch a thief. Besides being a little nervous, she really was very excited. Nothing this interesting had ever happened to her before, and she knew that if she lived to tell the tale - and she thought she probably would - it would be a good one. What made it even better was that she was with the two people, other than Holly, that she liked best in the world. Wouldn't Mrs. Shockley be impressed with the way her grand adventure was shaping up!

They had taken the bus from Oxford and, upon arrival at Victoria Station, checked into a small, discreet hotel just around the way called The King's Arms. They discussed their plans over lunch at the hotel and decided to approach Dr. Zanjani's flat under cover of darkness. That way, they were less likely to be spotted, and it would be easy to tell at a glance, from the lights, if anyone was home or not.

Their strategy was a simple one: Stake out Zanjani's apartment from the park across the street from her townhouse. If she wasn't there - go to Plan B, which was . . . well, they would decide on that later. At the first sign of darkness, Dr. Knight called a taxi and gave the cabbie a general address, "Pembroke Mews, please." They had determined that taking a cab would be more prudent than using the underground, where they might possibly run into Dr. Zanjani, and it was too far to walk.

Meriwether pressed her face close to the grimy back window of the cab and watched the lights of London smear past at a frightening speed. After what seemed like a very long time, the taxi pulled to a halt in front of a line of well-lit red brick townhouses with shiny black doors and neatly trimmed hedges. Bronze house numbers gleamed in the glow cast from the street lamps and bits of illumination peeked out from behind drawn curtains and pulled shutters.

"Very posh, this," said Daniel with a low whistle.

"Yes, I told you Samila enjoys the finer things in life," responded Dr. Knight. "Now, let's start walking like we know where we're going so no one gets suspicious. Number 16 is Zanjani. We'll cross the street up here and find a place to keep watch from."

The trio hid themselves in a dark spot between a tall hedge and a large elm. They were pretty well concealed, but if they heard someone passing by they could retreat even farther into the shadows. Each pulled a pair of tiny, high-powered binoculars (courtesy of Dr. Knight) from out their jacket pockets, positioning them toward #16 Pembroke Mews.

The binoculars, in reality, were not necessary. They could see perfectly well through the chinks in the hedge to the flat across the street, but the binoculars made them feel more like professional detectives and less like common peeping toms. Number 16 was dark as pitch.

"Now what?" asked Meriwether.

"Now we wait," replied her father.

And wait they did. It didn't take long for the novelty of spying to wear off and the boredom of inactivity to set in. Meriwether's knees were starting to ache from her crouched position. Daniel pulled a candy bar out of his pocket and started munching noisily.

"What!" he exclaimed at a particularly nasty look from Meriwether. "You wanna bite?" he asked, his mouth crammed with chocolate. Meriwether just rolled her eyes and shook out her legs a bit before changing positions. She checked her watch, 7:00. They had only been at it thirty minutes.

By 8:00, Daniel and Meriwether were ready to go back to the hotel and work on Plan B, but Dr. Knight showed no signs of wilting. They didn't dare say a word - for fear he'd regret bringing them at all, and at 8:42, by Meriwether's watch, his tenacity paid off. A sleek, black BMW pulled up to the curb in front of #16. A man with lots of perfectly styled white hair, dressed in a light blue button-down shirt and black slacks, got out of the car and walked around the front of the vehicle to open the passenger side door.

"That's the man from the airport!" exclaimed Meriwether. "The one I saw with Dr. Zanjani!"

A moment later, Samila Zanjani unfolded gracefully out of the beamer and allowed herself to be walked to her door. The man clicked a button on his key chain and the car's lights flashed with a quick beep. His alarm was set; he was going in. Lights flipped on in the downstairs front. Through the sheers they could see the two going into the kitchen at the back of the house . . . the binoculars were coming in handy now. Dr. Zanjani took two glasses from a cabinet and set them on the bar, while the mystery man filled them about a third of the way full with an amber colored liquid. He said something and she laughed. He helped her remove her wrap and lightly kissed her bare shoulder. Dr. Zanjani closed the curtains.

Dr. Knight cleared his throat, "Well, I've seen enough." His voice sounded strange in the darkness. "There's a tube station just across the park." Without another word, Dr. Knight stood up with a slight groan; he had been sitting in the same position for too long, and strode purposefully through the park.

Meriwether and Daniel followed a few paces behind. Meriwether was confused by her father's abrupt behavior. "You don't think he's still got it for her, do you?" she whispered to Daniel.

"Nah," replied Daniel sagely, "it's just a man thing. More likely he feels like throwing up."

The three rode in awkward silence back to their suite. Dr. Knight was clearly trying to work something out in his mind, and Meriwether did not like to interrupt. When they got to their rooms, Dr. Knight asked Meriwether to fill out the breakfast card for 8:00 a.m., patted her absentmindedly on the top of her head, and disappeared behind his bedroom door. Meriwether and Daniel stayed up for a while watching television until she noticed herself yawning and realized her eyes were watering with exhaustion.

"I'm going to bed," she said.

"Yeah, me too." Daniel got up and turned off the TV. "See you in the morning."

"8:00, bacon and eggs, waffles and fruit."

"Great." He quietly let himself into the room he was sharing with Dr. Knight.

Meriwether ran a scalding hot bath and poured in all the contents of a packet of sandalwood scented bath foam. She twisted her hair up and clipped it back, then sunk into aromatherapy heaven, letting her mind float. Images from the past few weeks sailed through her mind at random: doing the word jumble with Grandmother at the hospital, seeing her father on the front stoop that first evening in Oxford, riding bikes with Holly, watching rowers practice on the Isis, the little boy hugging his teddy bear on the plane, Mrs. Doone slumped over the kitchen table, the picture of her mother laughing, Daniel's grin ...She woke up with a start and realized she had fallen asleep in the bath.

Sleepily, she got out and wrapped herself in a fluffy white robe embroidered with The King's Arms crest. It was so long that it drug on the floor and the sleeves hung down about four inches past the tips of her fingers. Meriwether brushed her teeth and collapsed onto the bed. When she woke up at 7:45 the next morning she was in exactly the same position.

Meriwether didn't even want to know what her hair looked like - it had been damp when she had fallen asleep - so she knelt over the tub and gave it a quick wash. She combed it through, with only a little difficulty, brushed her teeth again and put on her white shorts and a black polo. When she stepped out of her bedroom, Daniel and her father were just sitting down to the breakfast she had ordered.

"Morning," smiled Dr. Knight, cup of coffee in hand.

"Morning," added Daniel through a mouthful of

waffle.

"Good morning!" chirped Meriwether, pouring herself a glass of orange juice and heaping her plate with a little of everything. "So, Dad, what's up?"

"What's up is I recognize the man we saw Samila with last night," answered Dr. Knight.

Meriwether and Daniel exchanged a look of surprise. "You do!" cried Meriwether. "But when I told you about him before, you said you didn't know him."

"Well, I don't really - know him, that is. When you gave me his description it didn't click, and even after I saw him last night I couldn't place it ...But I knew he seemed familiar somehow. I thought and I thought and I thought. Finally, I just went to sleep, and this morning, when I was shaving, it popped into my head! His name's Poole - don't remember the first name. He owns an antiques shop in Covent Garden. I met him on a dig in Israel probably 10 years ago. His hair was brown then."

"Do you know anything else about him?" Daniel wanted to know.

"He's smooth. Very smooth. Asks a lot of questions – but doesn't offer up much about himself. He can tell a fish story with the best of them!"

"What was he doing at a dig?" asked Meriwether, mentally placing herself at two years of age while her father swapped big ones in Israel with Poole.

"I've been wondering that too, actually. The question didn't occur to me at the time - I guess because everyone seemed to accept his being there as natural. He must have some connections in the archaeological field. He definitely has some now." Dr. Knight frowned into his coffee.

Meriwether Mystery   Emily Beaver

"So that's it, isn't it?" Meriwether began putting two and two together. "Poole and Zanjani are teamed up. They research and locate the artifacts they want, steal them, and then sell them . . . Black Market, like you said!"

"Sounds like it," nodded Dr. Knight.

"So, what's the plan?" asked Meriwether. "What do we do now that we know she's here in London?"

"I think we should check out Poole's shop . . . might be we'll find something interesting," Dr. Knight replied.

"But you can't go. What if he recognizes you? Worse, what if Dr. Zanjani is there?" worried Meriwether.

Dr. Knight paced slowly about the room. "You're right, I can't go. But I think it would be safe enough for you and Daniel. You can make a day of it. There's loads to see at Covent Garden. Shop, eat lunch, and act like tourists. Snoop around the shop, but don't draw attention to yourselves."

"Where will you be?" wondered Meriwether.

"I think I'll spend the day finding out a little bit more about this Poole fellow. Here, take this with you," Dr. Knight pulled something out of a canvas messenger bag that was sitting by the couch. "It's a walkie-talkie. I bought them yesterday. They have a two mile radius, so I'll keep relatively close.

"If you need anything – or get into trouble, just hold this button down here and talk into the speaker. I'll hear you."

Meriwether nodded as she took the walkie-talkie. She pressed the button and held it to her mouth, "Breaker, breaker. Over and out. Ten-four good buddy." Her words echoed out of the depths of the messenger bag as Daniel stifled a laugh. "Okay, good. So it works. Now, where do I put it?"

"Oh, I bought you this too." Dr. Knight dove into the messenger bag once again and fished out a black nylon fanny pack.

"I'm not wearing that!" announced Meriwether. "Daniel, you wear it."

"I'm not wearing it!" Daniel pushed away from the table and instantly put as much distance as possible between him and the offensive accessory.

"What's the big deal?" wondered Dr. Knight in genuine confusion. "I see people wearing them all the time."

"Fat people with 'I heart London' t-shirts and black socks pulled half-way up their calves!" exclaimed Meriwether. "I'm serious; I'm not wearing that!"

"Look, you can buy something else at Covent Garden to put the walkie-talkie in, but you've got to take it because we haven't got anything else," Dr. Knight reasoned.

"What about the messenger bag?" asked Meriwether.

"I need the messenger bag."

"You don't want to wear the fanny pack," wincing at the words, "either."

Dr. Knight just smiled as Meriwether grabbed the pouch and huffily buckled it about her hips.

"There you go," said her dad.

"It doesn't look so bad," said Daniel.

Meriwether rewarded them both with a terrific scowl.

Daniel and Meriwether took the tube to Covent Garden, a collection of shops and restaurants with an outdoor, market-like feel. Meriwether sat with her arms crossed against her middle and tried not to think about how stupid she looked. Daniel whistled amiably and ever so often looked over at her and grinned, his eyes twinkling. "So what should we do first?"

"Find a store, buy a bag, throw the fanny pack in the Thames," replied Meriwether through clenched teeth.

"Alright, alright . . . sheesh, girls!" Daniel shook his head in mock exasperation.

"Hey, you wouldn't wear it - so I don't want to hear it. Besides, I'm not the one walking around with the idiot tourist girl."

"Better than being the idiot tourist," laughed Daniel, dodging a swift right to the arm.

Meriwether quickly located a promising shop and discovered a darling Oriental themed purse with an extra long strap that she could wear securely over one shoulder and slung across her body - for added protection. Unfortunately, the purse was not big enough to hold the walkie-talkie, the notepad and pen she had taken to carrying about in order to jot down ideas and possible clues, and the fanny pack. Something had to go. Soon, Daniel and a much happier Meriwether set out on their day's mission. The unfortunate fanny pack lay discarded on a wooden bench, a necessary casualty.

"What now?" wondered Meriwether. "Maybe we should find a map. At home, there's always a kiosk in the middle of the mall that lists the stores and shows you where they are."

"This isn't a mall," replied Daniel.

"Well, it's kind of like a mall . . . an outside one."

"I've been here before, with me mum, and I've never seen a kiosk with a map on it. I think we're on our own."

"Okay, so let's get started. Remember, we're tourists and we're just shopping around."

"And if we happen to see Zanjani?"

"Hide."

Meriwether and Daniel spent a very pleasant morning trying on hats and admiring china. They sniffed tea and sampled biscuits. Meriwether bought them both a pair of sunglasses with some of the mad money her father had given her for the day, and they agreed that they looked very cool. They were checking themselves out in the small store mirror when Meriwether caught the reflection of a slim, dark figure with a swath of black hair passing outside. She elbowed Daniel sharply, "Did you see that?"

"See what?"

"I just saw Dr. Zanjani. Come on!"

They rushed out of the store and quickly caught sight of their prey. They watched as Zanjani made her way through the crowd and entered a small shop just a few doors down.

"That's gotta be Poole's shop," breathed Meriwether.

"I'm going in," announced Daniel.

"What!" Meriwether exclaimed.

"You want to hear what they're saying, don't you?"

"Well, yeah."

"And you can't go in because she'll recognize you, right?"

"Right."

"So, I'm going in," Daniel repeated. "She doesn't know me. I'll be fine. Who knows what we're missing while we stand out here and argue about it?"

"Alright," conceded Meriwether, "just be careful!"

"Right-o!"

Meriwether stood about nervously for what seemed like hours, but was actually closer to ten minutes. She turned quickly away as she saw Dr. Zanjani exit Poole and Assoc. and watched as Daniel emerged soon after, his expression unreadable.

"So, what'd you find out?" she blurted.

"Not much."

"What do you mean? What did you hear?"

"Nothing. They were in a back room the whole time. A girl was behind the desk. She asked if I looking for anything in particular? I said, a birthday present for me gran. She didn't bother me any more after that, but I couldn't get close enough to the door to hear anything they were saying. All I know is, when Zanjani came out, her eyes were shooting daggers."

"Do you think they know about Gerry?" Meriwether thought this couldn't be good.

"That'd be my guess. But who knows, really? Why don't you try your dad and see what he wants us to do now."

"Meet me back at the hotel and we'll compare notes," Dr. Knight's voice crackled out of the walkie-talkie.

Meriwether and Daniel took a pass by Poole and Assoc. before making their way to the tube station. The girl was still behind the desk - no sign of Poole.

"Something's going down. I can feel it," murmured Meriwether.

"You sound like Mum," grinned Daniel.

When Daniel and Meriwether got back to The King's Arms, Dr. Knight was waiting for them. They told him about seeing Zanjani at Covent Garden and about the backroom conversation. "We think she might know about

Gerry," said Meriwether.

"If she does, then we're running out of time," replied her father. "She'll disappear to Costa Rica or somewhere and we'll never catch her - or get Mother's box."

"So what did you find out about Poole? Anything?" asked Meriwether.

"Precious little," answered her father. "He's a real closed book. General consensus, though, is he's involved in some shady stuff. He's never been formally implicated in anything, but everyone agrees that he's got more on his plate than that antiques shop in Covent Garden."

"So it's like a front?" Daniel reasoned.

"Exactly," affirmed Dr. Knight.

"You think he and Zanjani have been together on this from the beginning?" wondered Meriwether.

Dr. Knight rested his elbow on the arm of his chair and thoughtfully rubbed the back of his neck. "That's what it looks like."

"So, what now?" said Daniel.

"Don't you think we should tell the police what we know?" Meriwether implored her father. She was afraid they were getting in way over their heads.

"I'd say you were right, except that we don't really *know* anything. That is, we don't have any real proof. Let me go a little bit further with this thing, Meriwether. I really feel that I've got to do it this way - without the police - if we're to have any chance of retrieving your Grandmother's box. And I, for one, don't want to go home without it."

Did he say, 'go home'? What did that mean, wondered Meriwether. *Did that mean go home to Oxford - or home to Texas? Was he planning to go back with her at the end of the summer? Was he coming back for good?* These thoughts raced through her mind and left her feeling a little dazed. When her mind was clear again, Daniel and her father were discussing the night's adventure.

"He's ...an old acquaintance of mine from my early days in London - when I first left home," Dr. Knight was saying. "He can get me in and out without setting off any alarms. You two can keep look-out."

"What are you talking about!" exclaimed Meriwether.

"Hello, earth to Meriwether," Daniel waved his open palms in front of Meriwether's face. "We're talking about breaking into Poole's shop."

"Tonight?!" Meriwether felt near hysterics.

"Yes, tonight." Dr. Knight appraised her curiously. "Where have you been, Meriwether?"

"Sorry, I - uh - sort of zoned out for a minute. But this is crazy! What if we get caught? We'll be arrested!"

"We won't get caught. Lenny is a professional. Besides, it's not all of us, it's just me and Lenny," answered her father with maddening calm.

"What do you mean, he's a professional?" Meriwether's eyes narrowed in suspicion. "You mean he's a thief?"

"Well, not any more . . . at least, I don't think. . . ." Dr. Knight dismissed the conversation with a backwards wave of his hand. "Anyway, we need him to do this because I don't know anything about alarms and all that, do you?"

"No."

"Well then . . . and it's not like we'll be stealing anything - anything that wasn't ours to begin with."

"What about *reformed* Lenny?" Meriwether wanted to know.

"I'll make sure he doesn't touch a thing," promised Dr. Knight. "Besides, you know what they say . . . it takes a thief . . ."

"To catch a thief!" Daniel and Meriwether recited in unison.

Chapter Fourteen

Against her better judgment, Meriwether helped her father prepare for the night's escapade. She and Daniel, as proposed, would keep watch outside the shop for passers-by. If worse came to worse, they would contact Dr. Knight by walkie-talkie and pretend to be teenagers, making out. Dr. Knight didn't like that idea, and mostly Meriwether didn't either, but it was the best they could come up with.

They all dressed in dark colors. Meriwether replaced her white shorts with black yoga pants and found herself wishing, for just a moment that she had the fanny pack back. It would have blended into the night better than the salmon pink of her new bag. Oh well, she told herself. Who would believe that a girl wearing a fanny pack would be making out with anyone, anyway?

At 10:00 there came a knock on the door, and Dr. Knight introduced Lenny to his two young partners in crime.

Lenny was, to Meriwether's surprise, a big hulk of a man. She was expecting a spry, cat burglar type. He had a grizzly face and twinkling blue eyes, and Meriwether judged him to be somewhere in his fifties. He might have been intimidating but for his voice. The homey Cockney tones set her immediately at ease.

"Good to meet you, good to meet you, young lass." Lenny shook her hand with ferocious good-will. "And there's a nice young lad for you," he said, taking Daniel's hand. Despite herself, Meriwether found that she liked him tremendously. "Leonard Downy, at 'yer service. But ye can call me Lenny, if an's you want."

Lenny carried a black satchel filled with a little bit of this and a little bit of that. As they walked, Meriwether eyed it suspiciously, sure that it would carry out a little bit more than it carried in. Daniel and Meriwether took their places in a shadowy corner where they could keep a good eye on the shop. Shivering slightly, whether from cold or nervousness she didn't know, Meriwether untied a slim, zippered sweatshirt from around her waist and shrugged into it. They both raised their tiny binoculars to their eyes, and the wait began.

Lenny and Dr. Knight approached the antiques shop cautiously. Lenny took something out of his bag and appeared to scan the storefront with it. The device beeped twice. Meriwether looked about wildly, sure the noise had given them away - but nothing happened. Apparently, this cleared them to go ahead. Lenny pulled some instruments from out his jacket pocket and proceeded to pick the lock. In no time at all, Dr. Knight and Lenny disappeared into the darkness of the shop.

Meriwether could see two small circles of light dancing around in the blackness - their flashlights. Presently, however, the lights vanished and she knew that the pair had let themselves into the back room where Poole and Zanjani had their tête-à-tête earlier in the day. Time drug by very slowly.

"What do you think they're doing in there?"

whispered Meriwether.

"Dunno," whispered Daniel back. "Who knows how big that room is or what's back there. They might even be trying to access computer files."

"Yeah, I hadn't thought of that." Daniel looked pleased with himself.

More empty minutes passed.

"Can I have a piece of gum?" wondered Meriwether.

"Um, sorry. I don't have any," answered Daniel, patting down his pockets.

"You're chewing gum!"

"It was my last piece . . . sorry!"

Big eye roll.

Without warning, Dr. Zanjani and Poole appeared outside the shop. Poole had his keys in hand and was preparing to unlock the front door.

"Quick!" exclaimed Meriwether in stage whisper. "It's them! Do something!"

Daniel looked around wildly for something that might create a diversion. There was nothing to knock over, nothing to throw. "Oy, over here!" he yelled.

"What are you doing?" hissed Meriwether.

Daniel shrugged apologetically," I dunno . . . sorry. Crikey! We'd better run for it!"

Dr. Zanjani was headed their way, something small and metallic in her hand. Poole had gone on into the shop. Daniel and Meriwether sprinted for the stairs. Meriwether was fumbling with her purse as she ran, trying to get the walkie-talkie out so that she could warn her dad. Even so, she realized it was probably too late. It had all happened so quickly.

They could hear Dr. Zanjani close on their heels as

they clattered down the stairway. At last, Meriwether managed to get hold of the walkie-talkie just as she tripped on the next to the last step and flew sprawling out onto the concrete. Daniel turned back to help her up, and Zanjani was on top of them, gun pointed.

"Are you all right, Meriwether?" asked Dr. Zanjani lazily. "That's right, dear boy. Help her up. That was a nasty fall, Meriwether. You should be more careful," a thinly veiled threat that was not lost on her audience.

"I wonder ...would you mind if I borrowed that?" Zanjani motioned toward the walkie-talkie with her revolver. Shaking with pain and fear, Meriwether handed it over. "Thank you, Meriwether." Whenever Zanjani spoke her name, Meriwether's blood ran cold. Zanjani held the walkie-talkie to her lips, suddenly business-like. "I've got the girl and her friend."

Daniel and Meriwether walked back up the stairs at gunpoint. Meriwether hoped Daniel was coming up with an escape plan because she didn't have a single thought in her head. The inside of her left hand, the one not holding the walkie-talkie, was bleeding. There was a hole in the knee of her new yoga pants, and the skin beneath was scratched raw. Meriwether observed these things, but she could no longer feel anything. It felt surreal. Like a dream.

As Zanjani marched them into Poole and Assoc., Meriwether noticed Daniel looking around the shop for some means of escape. Apparently, Dr. Zanjani noticed it too. "I wouldn't try anything if I were you. You are expendable."

Zanjani knocked lightly on the door to the back room and ushered her captives in. Meriwether was temporarily blinded from the unaccustomed brightness. When she recovered, she saw that Poole had her father and Lenny at gunpoint. Lenny's black bag of tricks lay slid across the floor out of reach. Meriwether and Dr. Knight exchanged a look that from her meant, "Sorry I let you down," and from him meant, "Sorry I got you into this."

"We keep running into each other, Peter," purred Dr. Zanjani.

Dr. Knight shot Zanjani a look of pure hatred. "What do you want, Samila?"

"I want a lot of things."

"What do you want from me? Surely you don't mean to kill us all?"

"Of course not, do not be silly. What I want, from you, is to be left alone. The gig is up, as you Americans say, and the time has come for Edward and me to fly. Let us fly, dearest Peter, and you may keep what is left of your little family. I will even let you have your precious box back. Am I not right to assume that is what this is all about?"

"The box means nothing. Give me Meriwether and I'll never bother you again." Dr. Knight was trying to stay calm, but Meriwether could read the terror in his eyes. *So this is what he meant when he said he was afraid to what lengths Zanjani might go.*

"Do not worry. No harm will come to the girl if you follow my instructions. I am curious you see, so curious. Tomorrow night we will meet again - I will let you know where. Do not be stupid, Peter. Tell no one of this. I will bring both your treasures ...you will bring the key. We will open the box together, you and I. It will be just like old times." Zanjani smiled, enjoying her part of the cat with its mouse. "Agreed?"

"Agreed." Dr. Knight assented with a steely glare and a set jaw. "Don't worry, Meriwether. You'll be fine. I promise."

"I know, Dad," Meriwether answered in a small voice, trying to be brave. She looked at Daniel. For once, he wasn't grinning. He looked like he'd just swallowed a really big pill.

"Touching," smiled Dr. Zanjani with a smile that could not reach her ice queen eyes.

"Now, if you gentlemen will kindly see yourselves back to The King's Arms, I'm afraid we're closed for business until tomorrow morning at 9:00," joked Poole in a fine Irish brogue. "I plan to be out of the country for a while, business and pleasure if you know what I mean, but if you're ever in the market for something special, say, for your *grandmother's birthday*, my assistant Janet is sure to be able to accommodate you. Good evening, gentlemen, it is so nice to see you again Dr. Knight." Poole escorted Dr. Knight, Daniel, and Lenny out of the store at gunpoint and watched them until they were well out of sight.

Returning to Zanjani and Meriwether, "Samila, my dear, our little one needs a bath and something to eat, I don't doubt. Shall we?" They each took Meriwether by an arm and walked her to Poole's beamer.

As she rode, securely buckled, in the back of Poole's car, Meriwether began to snap out of her daze and think clearly. Her first thought was that, surprisingly, she was not afraid. These people were not killers . . . or at least she didn't think they were. They were thieves. She was certain to be treated with every courteously during her one night of captivity, and she was sure that her dad would follow through with the conditions and not do anything 'stupid'.

Next, she thought about Poole's little speech and decided he had been bragging. He had purposefully revealed several things to impress upon them the scope of his information network. First, that he knew where they were staying. Second, that he knew about Daniel's visit to the shop earlier in the day. Third, no doubt an attempted jab at Dr. Knight, that he and Dr. Zanjani were a couple - not just partners. Her father had said that Poole played it close to the cuff, but Meriwether thought he might underestimate the capabilities of an 11, almost 12 year old girl. Zanjani and Poole had lots to discuss if they were leaving the country tomorrow.

Poole and Zanjani were arguing about what to pick up for dinner. Zanjani wanted Chinese. Poole wanted Indian.

When asked, Meriwether voted for Chinese. Triumphant, Zanjani dialed a number on her cell phone and ordered, *in Chinese*. Five minutes later, Poole parked the car in front of a dilapidated hole in the wall called Won-ton's. A green-glow fluorescent light illuminated cracked and peeling beige stucco and a duct tape mended front window. Poole got out to get their food. Zanjani shifted in her seat and trained her almost completely concealed pistol on Meriwether, "Won-ton's closes at midnight, and they don't deliver."

Five minutes after that, Zanjani, Poole, and Meriwether were sitting in Zanjani's kitchen devouring the take-out. Meriwether had absolutely no idea what she was eating, but she didn't care . . . it was delicious! Soon, Poole and Zanjani, full of food and conceit, began to relax. They asked Meriwether about her summer, and how she had liked this, or what she thought of that. It was as if they knew everything she had seen and done since arriving in England. But then, of course they did! They had been keeping close tabs on her, waiting for an opportunity to steal the key.

An involuntary shiver ran up Meriwether's spine. Up until now, she had not realized the scrutiny she had been under. Anger began welling up inside her, but she managed to keep it in check and answer their questions off-handedly, to put them at their ease. After a bit, Meriwether decided it was time to try and ask some questions of her own.

"So, why are you so interested in Dad's box? He told me there's just some sentimental stuff my grandparents gave each other in there. Nothing really worth anything like you'd be interested in."

Zanjani and Poole exchanged a look. "We think there may be more to this box than meets the eye," answered Dr. Zanjani, smiling enigmatically. "We are hoping that the key will help us to explore it more completely."

Okay, that's cryptic, thought Meriwether. Then out loud, "So you think there's something hidden in there? Some secret compartment or something?"

"Perhaps. Perhaps not. That is what I intend to find out tomorrow night."

"Do you have the box here? Can I see it?" asked Meriwether.

"Do you have the key?"

"No. Not anymore."

"Then you must wait until tomorrow; just as we

Meriwether Mystery   Emily Beaver

must wait." Zanjani stood up from the table. "Now I will show you to your room."

Meriwether followed Zanjani up to the third floor of her exquisitely decorated home. Everything was done in shades of white, cream, and taupe, and vases of fresh flowers adorned various pieces of dark, very expensive looking contemporary furniture.

"There is an en-suite bathroom, and some books for reading, so you should be quite comfortable. Do not attempt to go out onto the balcony or leave this room. I am setting the alarm for the night. I will bring your breakfast in the morning." As she said these things, Zanjani walked over to the bedside table and removed the telephone.

Winding the cord around its base, she continued, "As I said to your father, Meriwether, do not be stupid. We will all get what we want if everyone does exactly as I say. Do you understand?"

Meriwether looked deep into the dark pools of Dr. Zanjani's eyes. "I understand."

"Until tomorrow then. Sleep well." Zanjani closed the door, and Meriwether, her heart fluttering, reached out quickly and locked it.

"Now, what?" thought Meriwether, flopping down on the big bed, covered in ivory tone-on-tone silk stripes. She put her hands behind her head and stared up at the ceiling. Meriwether let her mind float, and, presently, found that she had come up with a plan. She took her notepad out of her purse and scribbled a quick list of things to do:

1. Look for some p.j.'s
2. Take a bath

3. Wash out undies in sink
4. Set watch alarm - 3 am.
5. Snoop around

Deet, deet! Deet, deet! Meriwether jolted awake and punched the button on her watch. She lay rigid for half a minute and let her eyes acclimate to the darkness, ears straining for any sound, any clue that someone had heard her alarm.

Nothing.

She got carefully out of bed, padded across the thick carpet in her bare feet, and peeked through the balcony curtains to the street below. Poole's car was gone.

Meriwether tip-toed back across the room to her door, unlocked it, and stood nervously with her hand on the doorknob. Zanjani had said that she was setting the alarm for the night, but surely that meant only for exterior doors.

She took in a deep breath and cautiously turned the knob. The door opened noiselessly with only the slightest bit of pressure. Meriwether blew out a sigh of relief as she slipped out, closing the door softly behind her.

When Zanjani brought her up the stairs earlier, Meriwether had noticed an office on the second floor. She thought this was a pretty good place to start, since she really had no idea what she was looking for. The only problem was the office was directly across the hall from the master bedroom.

Meriwether crept down the stairs, feeling extremely vulnerable in the too big satin cami and drawstring

Meriwether Mystery Emily Beaver

bottoms she had found in Zanjani's dresser drawer . . . especially since her underwear were still hanging on the shower rod in the bathroom upstairs. She shivered, and goose bumps popped up all over her body.

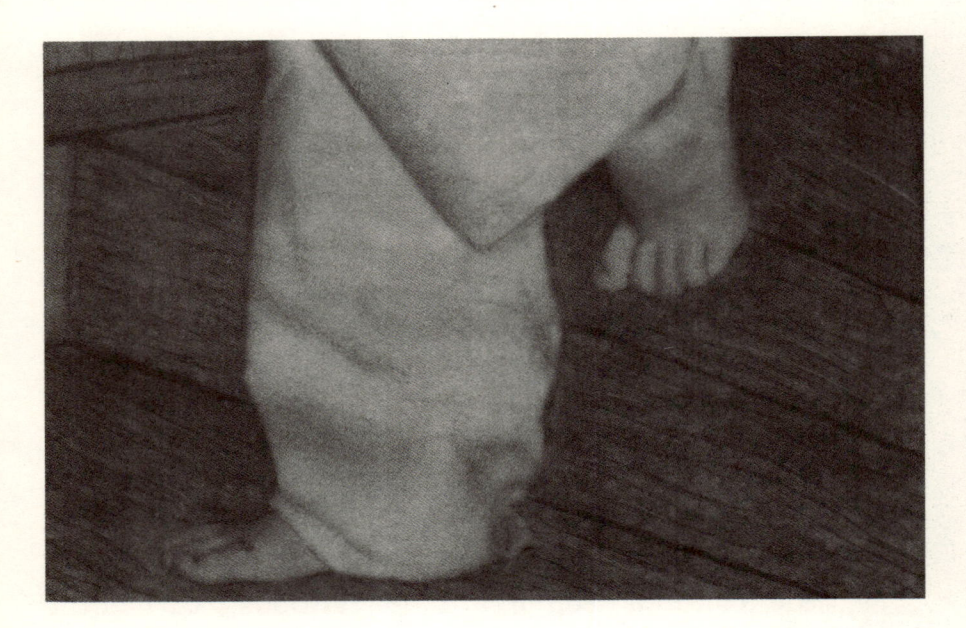

Then the unthinkable . . . she had to sneeze!
She froze on the steps and pressed the end of her nose with the tips of her fingers, scrunching up her eyes in concentration. After a few tense seconds, the tingling stopped, and she was able to continue down the stairs.
The door to the office was cracked open. Unfortunately, so was Zanjani's bedroom door. Meriwether stood still as a statue at the base of the stairs and, again, listened. She could just make out the gentle rumble of a snore coming from the bedroom.
She decided to go for it.

Meriwether Mystery   Emily Beaver

    Catlike, Meriwether slipped inside the office and closed the door behind her. Flipping the light on seemed like going a little too far, so she turned on the desk lamp and began carefully examining the contents of the desk. Nothing jumped out at her. A large file drawer at the bottom of the desk looked promising, but it was locked. Meriwether was fastidious about leaving everything the way she found it, remembering how she could tell that someone, namely Gerry, had been through her own things at her dad's.

    Meriwether was starting to get very cold, very disappointed, and very nervous . . . this was taking too long. She would just have to give it up and see what she could find out tomorrow.

    Just as she was getting up to leave, her elbow nudged the mouse to Zanjani's computer and the dark screen instantly came to life.

    Zanjani was still online!

    Meriwether hadn't even bothered with the computer because she thought she'd need a password. This was too good to be true! She quickly scanned the screen and noticed a shortlist of recent searches.

    Meriwether clicked on *Casa de Si*, the last search performed by Zanjani, and was instantly transported to a website showcasing a beautiful hotel. She read quickly:

> *The Casa de Sierra Madre, built in 1580 and exquisitely restored, is one of the finest small hotels in all Mexico. Situated in historic Santo Domingo. . . .*

    And then she heard it - a toilet flushing across the hall. She immediately clicked the X in the upper right hand corner of the screen, turned off the monitor and the desk light, and threw herself under the desk. Meriwether curled into a little ball and prayed that Zanjani would just go back to bed. She waited, knees held to chest, until her limbs started to cramp.

When she finally felt it was safe, Meriwether turned the monitor back on, let herself out of the office, and, losing her head, scampered back up the stairs to her room. Securely back inside, with the door locked, Meriwether dove under the covers and shivered there for awhile - waiting for her body to warm up and her heart to stop racing.

Chapter Fifteen

In spite of herself, Meriwether was awake by 8:00 the next morning. Her breakfast, however, didn't arrive until 10:00. Either Zanjani was a late riser, or Meriwether's stomach was not exactly at the top of her priorities today. Half a grapefruit and some buttered wheat toast would hardly fill her up, but beggars couldn't be choosers.

Meriwether thought about her dad and Daniel sitting at The King's Arms, waiting for the call from Zanjani to tell them where to make the exchange. She wished she could let them know she was okay. Their situation was actually much worse than hers because she knew she was fine - they didn't.

I could escape, thought Meriwether. She was sure she could do it if she wanted to, but the fact was . . . she didn't.

If she escaped, Zanjani and Poole would be gone and Grandmother's box would go with them. She would just have to play along with Zanjani and be a good little prisoner.

Because she had nothing better to do, Meriwether turned her thoughts to the night's meeting. She didn't trust Dr. Zanjani any further than she could throw her, and she *certainly* was not convinced that Zanjani would relinquish the box over to her father, as promised. A lot could go wrong.

Her mind spun with what-ifs and potentialities until she had given herself a splitting headache.

She found some aspirin in the medicine cabinet in the bathroom and took two. She opened the curtains to the balcony, and, on a whim, opened the balcony doors as well. Twenty seconds later, she heard a key fumble in the lock, and a breathless Zanjani flew into the room.

Meriwether turned and smiled from the edge of the balcony. "I just needed some fresh air. Don't worry, I'm not going anywhere."

Zanjani's eyes narrowed, "We meet tonight at 9:00. I see that you understand the situation and, perhaps, are curious also. Be careful, Meriwether. You know, of course, that curiosity killed the cat."

"Did it starve him to death? Because it's nearly 1:00, and I'm dying here."

"Tuna salad is served, mi' lady." Poole appeared in the doorway carrying a black lacquered tray, waiter-style. His blue eyes and white hair and teeth glistened in the sunlight thrown from the balcony. He set the tray down on the bed and escorted a scowling Zanjani out of the room.

Meriwether looked her tray over, pushed the tomato to the far side of her plate, demolished the tuna salad in under a minute and decimated her bottled water without ceremony.

"No wonder she's so skinny," grumbled Meriwether.

She was still hungry.

Time crept by very slowly that afternoon. Meriwether tried to take a nap, so that she would be at her best for whatever the night would bring, but she couldn't quite manage it.

She found some red fingernail polish and a pore reducing mask in the bathroom, so she painted her toenails and gave herself a facial. She stood on the balcony and watched people play with their dogs and their children in the park where she, Daniel, and her father had hidden just two nights ago. She observed Poole's BMW coming and going ...a lot. She paced the floor and halfheartedly thumbed through some of Zanjani's books.

At last, Zanjani knocked on her door. It was time to go. Zanjani handed her a package of granola bars and a soda. Poole met them in the kitchen, and once again, Meriwether was chaperoned into the car.

"Where are we going?" asked Meriwether, cramming a granola bar into her mouth.

Neither Zanjani nor Poole made any attempt to respond. They were both staring straight ahead, and the mood was tense. Meriwether wondered if they'd had a disagreement, or if they were just worn out.

Meriwether figured it out soon enough, anyway. They were going back to the antiques shop.

There were still a few people milling about Covent Garden. Shop owners were closing up for the evening and area restaurants were serving dinner.

They got out of the car and Zanjani flashed her revolver as a warning to Meriwether. Poole unlocked his shop, and Zanjani took Meriwether to the back room while Poole stayed in front to wait for Dr. Knight.

At 9:00 sharp, Poole brought Dr. Knight and Daniel into the back room. Dr. Knight immediately went to Meriwether, "Are you all right?"

"I'm fine, Dad. Are you all right?" Dr. Knight looked as if he hadn't slept or shaven since she'd seen him last.

"I'm fine, now."

Turning to Zanjani, Dr. Knight said, "Let's get this over with."

Poole took a key out of his jacket and opened a file drawer. He removed a rectangular object, wrapped in cloth, and set it down on a table in the middle of the room. Silently, Dr. Knight, Meriwether, Daniel, Poole, and Zanjani made a circle around the table.

Poole carefully unwrapped the box. Carved into the lid was a relief of Jesus praying in the Garden of Gethsemane. Around the outside of the lid were symbols that seemed, to Meriwether, strangely familiar.

"The key, Peter?" demanded Zanjani.

Dr. Knight produced the key from his shirt pocket and handed it to Zanjani. She held the key to the light, smiled, and then inserted the key into the lock.

She opened the box.

Inside were the objects that Dr. Knight had mentioned: a string of pearls enclosed in a velvet pouch, a pocket watch with an inscription on the back, "To Andrew on our first anniversary", Mr. Knight's Texas A&M college ring, plus a large aquamarine cocktail ring that Meriwether could not imagine her grandmother ever having worn. A slim drawer revealed a parcel of fragile letters, tied together with a bit of ribbon. Zanjani began to untie the ribbon but Dr. Knight objected.

"Those are private letters, Samila. They are not what you are looking for." Dr. Zanjani's eyes flashed briefly, but she laid the letters on the table along with the jewelry.

Hewn into the inside of the lid was another carving. This one of a woman, kneeling in front of a window, praying. The same strange carvings outlined this picture, and suddenly, Meriwether recognized them. They were the identical to the carvings that surrounded the West Door at St. Mary's. Meriwether looked at Daniel. She knew he had been to church with Mrs. Doone, but he didn't seem to have made the connection.

Zanjani ran her fingers lightly over the interior carving. She smiled greedily at Poole, "It was hers."

"Whose?" asked Dr. Knight.

Zanjani did not answer. Instead, she placed the key inside the lock, turned it counter clockwise, and rewrapped the entire parcel in the cloth.

"What's going on? I thought we had a deal," said Dr. Knight.

"The 'deal' is off," answered Zanjani. "Edward and I have a plane to catch, and you have an appointment with the authorities."

"What are you talking about?" shot Meriwether.

"Breaking and entering is a very serious offense, Meriwether. No doubt, Daddy will talk his way out of it. But by the time he does, we'll be sipping Margaritas."

"Hasta la vista, old mate." Poole drew his gun and the two backed out of the room, locking the door behind them.

This was exactly what Meriwether had been afraid would happen, and what had she done but stand there dumbly and let them get away with it!

She chanced a look at her dad, expecting to see a broken man, but instead she saw him listening with his ear to the door.

"What are you doing?"

"Thought she might pull something like this, so we enlisted a little help," answered Daniel.

Meriwether heard a scream and a gun shot, then another gun shot. A few seconds later, the door burst open and in staggered Lenny holding the box, his left shoulder bleeding. "Sorry mate, but they got away. Best get out of here before the police shows up. Sum-un's sure to 'ave heard the shots."

They gathered up the contents of the box from the table and hurried out of the shop. Dr. Knight helped support Lenny as they clambered down the stairs to the street below.

"Gar, if this don't sting!" winced Lenny, wedged between Daniel and Dr. Knight in the back of the taxi.

Meriwether sat in the front seat with the cabbie, cradling Grandmother's box in her lap. She twisted around in her seat, "What happened?"

"I was waitin' outside fer the two of 'em to come sneakin' out. I saw the lady was holdin' somethin' . . . figured it was what yer da' was after . . . so's I grabbed it. Must'a scared her, cause she screamed an' took off. Hollywood shot at me, nicked me shoulder, so's I shot back. Didn't get 'em though . . . me aim was off."

"Good thing you didn't get him. Then we'd be in a real mess," said Dr. Knight.

"Aye, yer prob'ly righ'," agreed Lenny.

"We're going to have to report this to the police, Dad. You do realize that, don't you?"

"Yes, Meriwether, I realize that. Best of luck to them ...finding those two. Like I said, they could be anywhere."

"I think I might know where they're going," said Meriwether, and she explained about the website she had found on Zanjani's computer. This clue, along with the Zanjani's hint about 'sipping Margaritas' and Poole's 'hasta la vista' had them at least convinced the pair was headed for Mexico.

Chapter Sixteen

They got Lenny's shoulder fixed up at the hospital, sent him home in a cab, and then took a different cab back to The King's Arms. Meriwether set the box on her night table and fell asleep, meaning to ponder it, but too tired to really think.

Next morning, Meriwether, Daniel, and Dr. Knight went to the police station and made their report. This took the entire day because they each had to give their separate stories about ten different times to ten different officers and detectives. Finally, they trudged back to the hotel, packed their things, and, although they had already forfeited another night's lodging, checked out and caught the night bus back to Oxford.

It felt so good to be back in her own bed in her own room! Again, Meriwether placed Grandmother's box on her night stand, and again, she fell straight to sleep without spending the time she wanted to spend thinking about it.

Next morning, Meriwether woke up to the comfortable smells of coffee percolating and bacon frying. Mrs. Doone was back! Meriwether rushed down the stairs in her pajamas and threw her arms around Mrs. Doone's middle. "I'll be back in five minutes . . . I'm just so glad to see you!"

Mrs. Doone giggled as Meriwether ran back up the stairs. She washed her face and brushed her teeth, ran a brush through her hair and pulled it back, and dressed quickly in shorts and a T-shirt. She shoved her feet into her flip-flops, and five minutes later, as promised, sat at the kitchen table swinging her legs and grinning from ear to ear.

"And what's got you into such a good mood this morning?" smiled Mrs. Doone as she placed a plate of bacon, eggs, and toast in front of Meriwether.

"I don't know, really," answered Meriwether. "I guess I'm just glad it's all over. I mean, we got Grandmother's box back, and nobody got hurt . . . well, except Lenny, but he's okay . . . ."

"Yes, Daniel told me all about Lenny," said Mrs. Doone, disapprovingly.

"Yeah, well, that's what I thought about him too - at first. But he turned out to be really nice, and if it weren't for him, you'd probably be bailing us out of jail right now instead of cooking us breakfast!

"Where's Dad, by the way?"

"He left early. Said there were some things he needed to do," Mrs. Doone replied.

Meriwether and Mrs. Doone ate their breakfast together and caught each other up. Meriwether told Mrs. Doone about their misadventures in London, and Mrs. Doone told Meriwether about her time at Irene's.

" . . . Well, I don't mean to be rude, but it is *so* good to be back in my own room. Irene's painted her guest room shocking green, of all things, and bless me if I couldn't see that color through me closed eyelids!"

Just as they finished breakfast, Daniel showed up to see if Meriwether wanted to go for a walk. As Meriwether went back to her room to change her shoes, she looked longingly at the box. What she really wanted to do was spend the morning concentrating on the carvings. There had to be more to it than met the eye.

Zanjani's words, 'it was hers,' kept running through Meriwether's mind. Who was 'her'? She felt sure that the markings were a clue, as was the carving on the inside of the lid. Meriwether had a feeling that Mrs. Doone might be able to help her figure it out, or at least steer her in the right direction. She also thought her father might know more than he was letting on.

Meriwether finished tying her shoes and patted the top of the box. "Later," she whispered.

But the walk with Daniel turned into an all day affair. He treated her to lunch; then they went to the Ashmolean to visit Dr. Knight, but he wasn't there, so they toured the museum without him. Meriwether was a little disappointed. She felt that going through with her father would have been more rewarding because he would know a little something extra about each piece - but, still, they had a good time.

By the time they boarded the city bus to take them back home, Meriwether was once again exhausted. Daniel walked her to the front door, and Meriwether went straight up to her room and flopped down across the middle of her bed.

One hour later, a knocking at her door woke her up. "Come in," she croaked, rolling over onto her back.

Dr. Knight stepped into the room and sat down on the bed beside Meriwether. "I heard you came by the museum today," he said.

"Yeah, we must have just missed each other. Its okay, Daniel and I had fun - but it would have been better if you'd been there."

"We'll do it again soon. You can never go through a museum like the Ashmolean too many times.

"I wasn't there because I was busy planning our evening," said Dr. Knight.

"What do you mean?" wondered Meriwether, sitting up.

"Surely you haven't forgotten? It's your birthday, Meriwether."

Meriwether's mouth dropped open. She *had* forgotten. How could she have? Well, there had been more important things going on. But the great part was, her dad *hadn't* forgotten!

"I asked Daniel to keep you busy today so I could throw something together. Happy Birthday, Meriwether," smiled Dr. Knight, taking a small wrapped box out of his pocket and handing it to Meriwether.

"Thanks, Dad!" Meriwether threw her arms around his neck. She noticed that his face was freshly shaven and he smelled delicious. Then she really looked at him and realized that he was dressed in a suit and tie. "What are we doing?"

"To celebrate the twelfth birthday of my one and only daughter, Daniel, Mrs. Doone, and myself are taking you to a fine restaurant, and then we are going to the symphony at the Sheldonian. Providential for us, your birthday fell on a Saturday because they usually have an event on every weekend, all summer long. The hard part was getting tickets on such short notice."

"But never mind all that. Open your present."

Meriwether opened the package with trembling fingers. Inside was cushioned an oval shaped locket suspended from a slender chain. A delicately tinted lily was etched into the rosy gold, and inside the locket were tiny black and white pictures of a baby on one side and of a young woman on the other. Tears filled Meriwether's eyes as she looked up at her dad.

"Thank you," she mouthed, afraid to speak.

"The baby is you, of course," explained her father hoarsely. "I gave this locket to your mother for Christmas, the first year you were born. I added the picture of Felicia," his voice cracked as he said her name, "today."

Meriwether Mystery   Emily Beaver

He cleared his voice, "Wear your fanciest dress. We'll meet you downstairs when you're ready. Dinner reservations are for 6:30."

When Meriwether could tear her eyes away from the locket, she hopped in the shower and let her hair dry naturally into loose curls. She put on a gauzy teal dress that tied at the shoulders and fell below the knee and clasped the necklace around her neck. Grabbing a lightweight cardigan, she took one last look in the mirror - *not bad*! - and skipped down the stairs.

Mrs. Doone, Daniel, and Dr. Knight were waiting for her in the kitchen. Mrs. Doone was wearing the same mauve suit she had donned for church the other morning, and Daniel, looking very uncomfortable, wore starched khaki pants and a white button-down shirt with a green and navy diagonal striped tie. He and Meriwether stood staring at one another for a moment.

They both said, "Wow, you look really nice," at the same time.

Meriwether blushed and turned her attention to Mrs. Doone. "You look really nice too, Mrs. Doone."

Mrs. Doone smiled, knowingly. "And you are a vision, Meriwether."

"And I already told you you looked great, Dad," Meriwether rushed, trying to avoid both Daniel and Mrs. Doone, "didn't I?"

"Well, maybe I didn't say it, but I thought it."

"Thank you, Meriwether," said her father brightly. "You are lovely."

"Thank you!" quipped Meriwether, feeling she'd suffered all the nice and politeness she could stand for one evening. "Happy Birthday to me! Let's go!"

The restaurant her father had chosen was a little back alley cafe in the upstairs of one of the many centuries old buildings of Oxford. They had taken the bus to just shy of City Center, and then walked from there to Ma Belle's.

The inside of Ma Belle's was painted a rich shade of terra cotta, and the walls were hung with black and white photographs framed in black. Fresh flowers and lit votives graced tables dressed in white linen. The maitre-de led them to their table, and they were waited on by a somber little man with a snowy apron tied crisply about his waist.

Meriwether feasted on spinach crepes and chocolate torte for dessert. The food was divine, but even better was the company.

By the end of dinner, faces were flushed, eyes were bright, and all were having a very good time. Daniel, over his initial discomfort, held out his arm for Meriwether as they crossed the few blocks to the Sheldonian for an evening of Bach, while Dr. Knight escorted a giggling Mrs. Doone into the domed theatre.

The Sheldonian was shaped like a Greek amphitheatre, with stadium seating up and out from the performance platform which sat at ground level in the middle of the hall. They arrived to the discordant sounds of musicians tuning their instruments, and Meriwether felt her heart do a funny leap. As they took their seats, the lights dimmed and the concert began.

The music was so beautiful; Meriwether felt her heart would break. Never in her life had she heard live music of this caliber. Daniel nudged her gently with his elbow and handed her a handkerchief. Meriwether, realizing that tears were running down her face, smiled gratefully at Daniel as she dabbed at her cheeks.

It had been the perfect celebration Meriwether had always dreamed of. Her only regret was that Holly had not been there to share it. When she got home that night, Meriwether wrote Holly a long letter detailing the experience, lamenting the miles that separated them. Finally, close to midnight, Meriwether's head dropped back against her pillow. She looked at the box, *tomorrow*, she thought, and fell asleep saying her prayers.

Chapter Seventeen

The next two weeks flew by for Meriwether. Dr. Knight took some time off from the museum and rented a little car to tour the rolling hills and postcard villages of the Cotswolds with Meriwether. They even ventured up into the Lake District and on into Scotland and its capital, Edinburgh. This was a wonderful time for Meriwether because she was finally getting to spend some quality time with her father. And, little by little, he began to talk about her mother.

"I met your mom at Oxford, you know," he began one day as they drove precariously along a narrow road, dark trees dotting the hillside to their right; to their left, a low stone barrier all that separated them from plummeting to certain death in the blackness of the lake below.

"Oh, really?" replied Meriwether through clenched teeth, determined not to let on how terrified she was. Another car zipped past them within mere inches. Meriwether gripped the edge of her seat. Dr. Knight appeared not to have noticed.

"She was a member of OUDS . . . Oxford University Dramatic Society . . . they were performing a production of *Romeo and Juliet*. Felicia was *Juliet*. She was amazing! I waited out front to meet her after it was over and invited her to have a picnic with me the next day. She accepted . . . and the rest is history."

"So y'all were one of those cute couples I see picnicking along the Isis," smiled Meriwether, conjuring a picture of her mom and dad, spread out on a blanket along the banks of the river.

"Yes, that became one of our favorite things to do. I was quite a bit older, you see. I was already apprenticed at the Ashmolean, working on my doctorate. Felicia was only twenty when we met. Twenty-one when we married."

"Wow, that's really young!" exclaimed Meriwether.

"Too young, probably. I certainly wouldn't want to see you married at that age. Her parents were opposed to the match, partly for that reason . . . but we were in love. I'd already alienated my family, and she decided to go against hers. It was just the two of us against the world."

"Sounds romantic," sighed Meriwether.

"Yes, sounds that way doesn't it?" Dr. Knight careened around a sharp corner, showering pebbles down the cliff face. "The truth is Felicia never got over it. Especially when you came along and she got so sick. She really needed her family."

"They never forgave her?"

"No."

"How horrible!"

"Yes." Dr. Knight's jaw was tight; his knuckles white as they gripped the steering wheel. They drove in silence for some time. Meriwether was afraid to say anything.

Eventually, the muscles in Dr. Knight's face and arms began to relax. They pulled to a stop at a pub in a little town at the base of the hill. He stepped out of the car, took a deep breath and stretched. The breeze ruffled his hair and his cotton shirt, and Meriwether was struck with how handsome he was.

He leaned down into the car, an apologetic half-smile on his face, "Sorry about that. Are you hungry? I promise to be good company."

"Are you kidding? I'm starving!" said Meriwether, relieved that his dark mood had passed. She jumped out of the mini, linking her arm through her father's.

When they arrived back in Oxford, Dr. Knight was at once very busy with the million and one things that had piled up during his absence and Meriwether realized, with a start, that she had only two weeks left before she was scheduled to return back to Texas. Time was running out, and she hadn't figured Grandmother's box out yet. The time had come talk to Mrs. Doone.

She found her polishing the furniture in the tiny dining room. "Mrs. Doone?"

"Yes, dear."

"I need your help with something."

"Oh, and what is it now?"

Meriwether set the box down on the dining room table. "I'd like you to look at this box and tell me what you see."

Mrs. Doone lifted her glasses from her chest and leaned over the box. She squinted at the carving for a moment, and then said, "Would you mind if we took it into the kitchen? The light's so much better in there."

"Sure!" Meriwether lifted the box and carried it to the kitchen table. Light poured in from the big bay window as Mrs. Doone once again studied the box.

After a while, Meriwether said, "Now look inside."

Mrs. Doone opened the lid and turned her concentration to the relief of the woman. Meriwether saw her brows knit. And as she watched Mrs. Doone run her fingers over the characters that bordered the carving, she knew that Mrs. Doone had made the connection.

"I'm no scholar, but I can tell you one thing," began Mrs. Doone, "this box has something to do with St. Mary's. These carvings are identical to the ones surrounding the West Door . . . but I guess you noticed that."

"Yes, but what does it mean?" wondered Meriwether. "When Dr. Zanjani saw the inside of the box she said, 'it was hers.' Who is 'her'?"

"Again, I'm not an authority," Mrs. Doone's eyes shone with excitement as she pointed to the woman's likeness, "but I'm thinking this might be Annora!"

"Annora?"

"Annora, the anchoress of Iffley Church."

Meriwether was still confused. "What's an anchoress?"

"An anchoress is a recluse," explained Mrs. Doone, her fingers gently exploring the details of the carvings. "In medieval times, a noble woman whose family had fallen out of favor with the court would sometimes seek asylum with a church. There's a pamphlet that tells all about it. Annora's cell has recently been discovered and we're in the process of renovating it and getting it ready for public viewing. That's what the fund raising has been about.

"Come with me to church tomorrow. I'll call someone up and have them give us a tour."

"That would be awesome!" cried Meriwether, and in a more cautious tone, "But maybe you shouldn't tell them *why* we want to see it just yet."

"Sure and my lips are sealed." Mrs. Doone zipped her mouth closed, locked, and threw away the key.

Later that day, Daniel stopped by to deliver some groceries and catch up with Meriwether. They sat in Dr. Knight's study, the box set in front of them on the shining mahogany coffee table, as Meriwether explained to Daniel her theories about the nature of the vessel.

"Yeah, now that you mention it, I do recognize these carvings," said Daniel, running his fingers around the perimeter of the box, just as his grandmother had done. "If it really belonged to her, Annora I mean, what do you think that means? Like, how did your family come to have it? Do you think you're related?"

"I don't know what it means. I know that Grandmother has a family history at home, but I have no idea if it goes back that far. If it doesn't, I don't know how we could ever really know for sure," replied Meriwether.

"I wonder if there's some way to find out about Annora before we go to church tomorrow?" wondered Daniel as he carefully lifted the lid.

"You're coming with us?"

"You just try and stop me," he grinned, chocolate brown eyes glinting with excitement.

"Well, I guess we could try looking it up on the computer." Meriwether stood and walked over to her father's desk. She plopped down in his tufted leather swivel chair and keyed in his password, 'FelMer.' Daniel stood behind her as she typed 'Annora, Iffley' into the search engine. They were directed to the site for St. Mary's in Iffley Village. Voila!

"ANNORA THE ANCHORESS, THE RECLUSE OF IFTELE," read Meriwether. She hit print and read aloud from the screen as Daniel perused the pages coming out of the printer.

"Church annals dating from the thirteenth century allude to an enigmatic figure called Annora, the anchoress, who lived out the last years of her life enclosed in a cell beside St. Mary's. An anchoress is a recluse - someone who lives secluded from other people . . . ."

"I *can* read, no matter what Gran thinks," joked Daniel.

"Oh, yeah, sorry," smiled Meriwether, flushing.

Through their individual - *silent* -reading they learned that Annora, born in the late 1100s, was the daughter of William de Braose, a powerful baron in the reigns of Richard the 1st and King John - of Robin Hood lore. He'd held extensive lands along the border between England and Wales. Early in John's questionable reign, Annora's father was a supporter, but in 1207 a quarrel arose between them and John avenged himself upon the entire De Braose family.

William de Braose was outlawed. His wife, Mathilda, and Annora's oldest brother were imprisoned in Windsor Castle and left to starve. Annora's sister, Loretta, and her husband Giles fled to France; their lands were seized. Annora and four young nephews were imprisoned in Bristol Castle.

Annora's release was ordered in 1214. Her husband, Roger Mortimer, died in 1227. They had no children.

Meanwhile, her sister Loretta had retired to a cell in Canterbury. In 1232, Annora followed suit and came to Iffley, thereby placing herself under the protection of the Bishop, agreeing to remain in her cell until her death.

"Wow, that's some pretty wild stuff," said Daniel,

letting out a low whistle.

"Yeah," agreed Meriwether. She looked at Grandmother's ...or was it Annora's? ...box with new reverence. "I've read lots of books about *King* John. I always thought he was a real jerk, but it never hit quite so close to home, you know?

"I mean, can you imagine throwing a person's entire family in jail to rot?"

"No wonder she became a recluse," said Daniel. "She was probably scared to death."

"Do you really think it was hers?" asked Daniel with a sideways nod of his head toward the box.

"I don't know. I guess I want to believe it was, but I don't know how to prove it."

"Have you talked to your dad about it?"

"No, but I think I should. He obviously had some ideas about its origin. Maybe he knows when it was made."

Daniel smiled, "If I know your dad, he knows more than you think. Where is he now?"

"He's at the museum. Do you think we should bother him?"

The two stared at one another for a hanging second.

"Definitely," they agreed.

Chapter Eighteen

It was another gray, drizzly day, so Meriwether ran upstairs to stow the box -- she still didn't trust Zanjani and did not want to leave it laying about -- grabbed her jacket, and pulled her frizzing hair into a loose knot. They called to Mrs. Doone that they'd be back in a bit and stood impatiently about at the bus stop while little drops of moisture formed on their noses and caught in their hair.

At last, the bus screeched to a stop in front of them. They waited for the little old Indian lady to dismount the steps, laden as usual with her small, smelly bag of groceries. She nodded at Meriwether and Daniel as she passed, smiling broadly to reveal a mouth full of large yellow teeth. Meriwether noticed that her skin was as smooth as a 20 year old. Returning the smile, they scampered up the steps and found a seat right behind the driver.

The bus delivered them directly to the Ashmolean, and the two half ran to the street level entrance. Daniel wrenched the heavy metal door open and held it for Meriwether. Once again, Meriwether found herself in the lifeless corridor, but this time she knew where she was going. They knocked at the storage room door, but there was no answer, so they let themselves in. The storage room was dark, but they could see lights on in the lab.

"Dad?" called Meriwether, not wanting to catch him unaware. Again, no answer, but they soon found him perched on a stool he had pulled up to one of the lab tables, hunkered down over an object he held in his left hand while his right hand gently swished at the artifact with a fan shaped brush. "Dad."

Dr. Knight gave a start, fumbling precariously with the article. "Meriwether, Daniel! What are you two doing here?" He held his hand to his heart, looking at them sternly over the tops of his spectacles. Meriwether suddenly lost her nerve and wished she had left him alone and saved her questions for later that evening.

Daniel sensed her hesitancy, "It's about your mother's box, sir. We think we know who it belonged to . . . originally, I mean."

"Whom it belonged to."

"What?"

"You said 'who it belonged to,'" explained Meriwether. "It should be 'whom it belonged to.'"

Daniel looked at her like she was losing her mind.

"Sorry, never mind." Muttered Meriwether, her color rising.

Dr. Knight chuckled as he swiveled around on his stool, giving them his full attention. "Go on."

"You tell him Meriwether. You're the one who . . . whom . . . oh, bollocks! You're the one that figured it out."

"Well, I didn't really," clarified Meriwether. "I just recognized the markings from when I went to church with Mrs. Doone that one time. She's the one who told me about Annora."

"Ah, yes," smiled Dr. Knight surreptitiously, "so you

know about Annora."

Daniel and Meriwether just stared at him. "You know about Annora?" Meriwether fairly accused. "Why didn't you say anything?"

Dr. Knight turned his attention back to the object he held, the cleaning brush swishing methodically back and forth against the recondite form. "I thought you might figure it out."

"So you've known all along?"

"Oh, no . . . not all along. But you must remember I've had a lot of time to think about this. That box represents my shame and my redemption. It has never been far from my mind, these 25 years.

"Felicia and I were married in St. Mary's ...Did you know that, Meriwether?"

Meriwether shook her head dumbly.

"I know the church well. Of course, I'd never heard of Annora . . . but when the cell was discovered, I began to suspect there might be a connection . . . the time period was right at any rate.

"I've been doing some research on the subject. Would you like to see what I've put together so far?"

Laying the object aside, Dr. Knight strode to his office and rummaged through a large filing cabinet as Meriwether nodded, the capability of speech momentarily having escaped her. In a wink, Dr. Knight was back toting a lidded, brown manila file folder, the band straining against the bulk it contained.

"Be my guest," he offered, plunking the folder down on an adjacent lab table.

Dr. Knight resumed his task as Meriwether and Daniel poured over the mountain of obscure information her father had accumulated. Dr. Knight had transcribed most of the documents, but some of the text was almost completely indiscernible. Of particular interest was a letter, dated March 13, 1262, in which the son of Lorraine and Giles, Annora's nephew, wrote to his mother, detailing a visit he received from the deceased Annora's handmaiden.

"...and she delivered to me moste graciously the treasures laid upon our sister by our king and protector. Among them, a compartment of such exquisite detail as has aught been my pleasure to behold, her image carved therein..."

"This is it!" cried Meriwether, "This has to be it!"

"Sir, does this mean your ancestors were the De Braoses?" asked Daniel.

"Yes, I think so, Daniel," answered Dr. Knight. "If you'll look in the back of the folder, you'll find a family tree I've attempted to put together."

Meriwether found the tree and smoothed it out on the table in front of them. Dr. Knight, abandoning all pretenses, came up behind them to guide them through it.

"There are a few holes, but, with reasonable certainty, I believe I can trace our family back to the De Braoses through Annora's Norman mother, Mathilda," explained Dr. Knight excitedly, rifling through the documents. "Our line actually traces to this nephew of Annora's who received the box after her death."

"That's amazing," breathed Meriwether.

"Cool," nodded Daniel.

Meriwether thought out loud, "So that's why Zanjani wanted it so badly! It's a real archaeological find, isn't it?"

"Well there's that," murmured Dr. Knight, his head buried in the manila folder, ". . . and the treasure."

"The what?" exclaimed Meriwether and Daniel, looking at one another to make sure they had both heard the same thing.

"The De Braose treasure," answered Dr. Knight calmly, the corners of his mouth betraying the hint of a smile.

The air hung thick with anticipation. Meriwether and Daniel stared intently at Dr. Knight, their faces silently pleading with him to continue. Dr. Knight grinned, and then with a chuckle added, "Legend holds that Annora escaped with and concealed a portion of the family jewels, in particular, a magnificent necklace belonging to her mother.

"A portrait of Mathilda, wearing the necklace, hangs upstairs...Want to see it?"

Moments later, Dr. Knight, Daniel, and Meriwether were standing in a polished exhibit hall, gazing at a portrait of a proud beauty with very fair skin and volumes of dark, curling hair. The necklace hung close about her slender neck. Two strands of pearls met in a glittering oval cut emerald, the size of a large beetle. The stone lay ensconced in a bed of shimmering diamonds.

"Yeah, this is definitely more Zanjani's style," said Daniel.

"Definitely," agreed Dr. Knight.

Meriwether checked to make sure they were alone, then whispered, "But where's the necklace? It's not in the box, unless there's some hidden compartment I haven't discovered yet."

"Well, there's always that possibility . . . ," answered her father in low tones, "regardless, I think somehow the box holds the clue to where the jewels, Mathilda's necklace included, are hidden." With a broad smile, he continued, "You only have a few weeks left, Meriwether. You'd better get busy."

Chapter Nineteen

Meriwether and Daniel took the bus back to her father's house; she had almost begun to think of it as home, but her father's words, *you only have a few weeks left*, had jarred her in more ways than one. She was anxious to decipher the secrets the box held, and she always felt she worked better under pressure. At the same time, however, an awful empty feeling had settled in the pit of her stomach. Two weeks. Two weeks, and she would return to her **real** home: to Grandmother, to Holly, to small town West Texas and 7th grade. That was her life. Not this. And her dad didn't even seem upset to be losing her! Even if she were able to come back next summer, that was a whole year! And what about Daniel? Things could be totally different by the next time they saw each other. What if he had a girlfriend and didn't even want to hang out?

"Hey," nudged Daniel with his elbow, "what's wrong?"

Meriwether, jolted out of her reverie, forced a smile and lied, "Nothing."

"You'll be back," smiled Daniel, knowingly.

"What?" Meriwether pretended not to know what he was talking about.

Daniel, with his uncanny ability to read Meriwether's mind, continued, "You'll be back before you know it. Why don't you ask your dad if you can come home for Christmas?"

Home? Suddenly, Meriwether felt much better. She returned his smile, and this time it was genuine.

"Yeah . . . Christmas." Christmas in Oxford would be beautiful! Meriwether had never seen a white Christmas before. Sure, it had snowed . . . but never more than an inch or so. Some years it didn't snow at all -- and never at Christmas. "I'd like that."

"Here we are then," Daniel popped up from his seat as the city bus rolled to a stop. Meriwether gathered up her thoughts and herself and followed him off the bus. A group of kids had set up an impromptu game of soccer on the rugby field. They screamed with delight as they pelted up and down the field. A quick check of traffic, and Meriwether and Daniel sprinted across the street, down the sidewalk, through the painted white door of #240, "We're home!", and up the stairs to Meriwether's room.

Meriwether carefully pulled the box out from under her bed and set it on the comforter directly between the two of them. They spent the next few hours going over every square inch of the box, inside and out. They pushed and prodded the carvings, trying to trigger the release on hidden compartments. They studied the markings around the edges of the lid, looking for secret messages . . . nothing doing. At last, Daniel stood up and announced in a defeated sort of voice, "I've got to go home. I promised Mum I'd eat dinner with her and what's his face tonight." Daniel made a face, and Meriwether laughed.

"Why don't you like him?"

"I dunno," Daniel shrugged.

"Your mom likes him, though . . . right?" Meriwether asked hesitantly. Keeping her eyes on the box, she watched Daniel with her peripheral vision.

"I guess," grunted Daniel, averting his eyes as well.

"Okay, well, church in the morning then. I'll make a rubbing of these symbols and we can compare them with the actual door. Maybe there's a clue there."

"That's a good idea," answered Daniel in a distracted sort of way. "Yeah, okay . . . I'll meet you here in the morning. See ya," he waved absently.

"Bye," said Meriwether, smiling in what she hoped was a normal way. What was up with that? One minute, Daniel had been busily intent on the box -- next minute, all remote and depressed like. She knew it must be something to do with the guy his mom was seeing, but being as how she was unable to read his mind as he seemed to be able to read hers, she figured she'd just have to wait until he was ready to talk about it. She shrugged her shoulders in a rolling sort of motion, closed her eyes and stretched her neck deliciously from one side to the other, then concentrated her attention on the task at hand.

Next thing she knew, her father was standing over her, pulling a quilt up around her shoulders. Her room was dark except for the light coming in from the hallway. "Did I miss supper?"

Her dad chuckled, "Yes, you did. Mrs. Doone made you a plate and put it in the fridge. You can warm it up in the microwave if you're hungry."

"What time is it?"

"9:00. I'm going up to my studio. Thought I'd take a go at Annora's box, if you don't mind."

"Yeah, here take it," yawned Meriwether handing him the box. "We didn't find anything, but we're going into Iffley tomorrow morning with Mrs. Doone. I've made a rubbing of the carvings to take with us." She turned on the bedside lamp and handed him some papers lying on the night stand. "You want to go with us?" she added hopefully.

Dr. Knight hesitated. "We'll see," he answered at last. "Are you getting up or going downstairs to eat?"

Meriwether yawned again and pulled the quilt up closer under her chin. "I think I'll just stay put. If I get up now, I'll never get back to sleep."

"Okay," smiled her father, bending down to kiss her forehead. "Good night."

Meriwether closed her eyes, relishing his somewhat whiskery kiss, "Good night, Dad."

He took the box and closed the door softly behind him. Meriwether closed her eyes again; hoping she would be able to drift back into sleep, but there was much too much to think about. An hour later, her tummy grumbling distantly, Meriwether gave up and swung herself out of bed. She warmed up the shepherd's pie Mrs. Doone had left for her and finished with a large slice of chocolate cake and glass of milk.

She took a bath and slipped into her p.j.'s, but she still wasn't sleepy, so she sat at the writing desk in her room and composed a long letter to Holly telling her all the latest breaking news. She thought about Holly as she wrote, imagining her spending lazy days at the swimming pool, her skin getting tanner, her hair getting blonder -- and evenings playing basketball and board games with her brothers. Holly had written a few times over the summer, but her letters were oddly short and uninformative -- odd because Holly could **talk** a blue streak. Meriwether wondered who she was hanging out with. Sometimes Holly would write something about *we did this* or *we did that* . . . but she never explained who *we* was. Even though she didn't want to believe it, Meriwether worried sometimes that over the summer she had been replaced.

Three pages later, Meriwether folded the thick white sheets of stationery and tucked them into a matching envelope, licking it closed. She addressed the envelope and wrote "Air Mail" diagonally across the bottom left corner, turned off the desk lamp, and crawled into bed. Sleep did not come easily, but she stuck with it and eventually drifted off.

Next thing she knew, her father, dressed in pressed slacks and a crisp white shirt, was shaking her gently awake. "Time to get up, sleepy head."

"What? . . . Oh, you're going!"

"Yes," he said simply.

"Great! What time is . . ." Meriwether squinted at her watch, sleep still clouding her eyes, "Oh my gosh!"

"Yes, sorry," Dr. Knight scrunched up his face, "Daniel's downstairs . . . and we got to visiting . . . and the time sort of got away from us," he ended feebly.

Meriwether leapt out of bed. "Daniel's already here?" she yelped. "Okay, I can do this. I can do this . . ." she muttered to herself. "Gimme five minutes!"

"You can take at least ten," answered her father grinning. And with a withering look from Meriwether he added with a chuckle, "You look just like your mother."

Chapter Twenty

It was a merry little party that wound its way to church that morning. Daniel and his gran walked arm in arm, and Meriwether munched hungrily on the muffins Mrs. Doone had packed for her. The air was crisp and clean. Dr. Knight didn't say much, but looked about with a secretive smile on his face, as if his mind was filled with happy memories of past visits to Saint Mary's and the little village of Iffley. They'd planned it so they would arrive early in order to study the West Door in peace. They all felt the need for secrecy at this point and wanted to avoid questions from well-meaning parishioners.

The village was quiet as they approached the church. They did not see a soul. Mrs. Doone pulled Meriwether's rubbings out of her handbag and handed them to Dr. Knight. Dr. Knight positioned himself about ten feet back from the West Door and held the rubbings out so that if they stood behind him, they could all study and compare the symbols from the rubbing with the symbols surrounding the door. It was very difficult. The carvings were tiny from this distance, and some were quite intricate. The sun was shining brightly in the sky at this point, and Meriwether could feel the prickle of sunburn on her cheeks and shoulders.

They stood there for a good long time until Mrs. Doone whispered, "Someone's coming."

She strode purposefully toward the approaching couple as Dr. Knight quickly folded the rubbings and stuffed them in his back pocket. "Good mornin' to you Reverend March, Virginia."

"Good morning, Effie!" answered Reverend March. "You've brought a right crowd with you this fine Lord's day." Reverend March was short and slight and had the kindest pale blue eyes Meriwether had ever seen. His graying hair was receding mightily. He removed his spectacles and wiped the lenses, and then his large forehead, with his handkerchief.

"Why are you all here so early?" asked Virginia March pointedly, a calculating expression on her face. She was tall and thin, with long, strong limbs and a no-nonsense, boy-short haircut, which seemed to suit her. Meriwether thought instantly that there wasn't much getting past her and was reminded irresistibly of Aunt Phil.

Mrs. Doone looked back nervously, reluctant to tell a blatant lie to her pastor and his wife. Dr. Knight stepped in, "Just reliving some old memories, Virginia." Meriwether smiled brightly, suspecting her father had revealed a good deal of his own truth. "How are you, Alan?" continued Dr. Knight, holding out his hand and walking toward Reverend March. "It's been a long time."

"A long time, yes," smiled Reverend March kindly. "Too long.... We've missed you, Peter."

"Thank you," said Dr. Knight, but Meriwether had a feeling that they were saying a lot more than the rest of them could hear.

"Virginia, dear, this is Meriwether . . . Dr. Knight's daughter . . . remember, I told you about her earlier in the summer," rambled Reverend March in the way of introductions.

"Of course I remember," responded Mrs. March briskly, striding forward and taking Meriwether's hand in a forceful grip. "I'm sorry I missed your first visit. I was with my sister in Dover."

"Nice to meet you," said Meriwether, not knowing what else to say. She had the uncomfortable feeling that she was being sized up. At this moment, however, she was spared further appraisal by the arrival of more church members. Reverend and Mrs. March were at once busy with their responsibilities of meeting and greeting. Meriwether, Daniel, Dr. Knight, and Mrs. Doone snuck away, finding their way into the church building and Mrs. Doone's regular pew.

"That was a close one," murmured Mrs. Doone. "Virginia March doesn't miss a beat."

Dr. Knight responded with a wink and an enigmatic smile.

"Did you see anything?" Daniel whispered to Meriwether. "I could hardly see those symbols. Maybe I need glasses," he added in horrified tones.

"You don't need glasses," muttered Meriwether, "I couldn't see much either, but it has got me to thinking …"

"Thinking what?" wondered Daniel.

Meriwether looked about furtively. People were taking their seats, visiting, not paying them the slightest bit of attention. "Thinking that whomever carved the box . . . especially if it was a gift from *King Henry*," she mouthed the words, "would either have had to sit right there in front of the West Door in order to create an exact replica . . . or else the symbols aren't supposed to be a perfect match . . . just a representation . . . you know what I mean?"

"Yeah, I think so," nodded Daniel. "You mean we were looking for the wrong thing."

"Yeah, maybe . . . I don't know, it's just an idea. I'll run it by Dad later." Dr. Knight, sitting on the outside of the pew, was shaking hands with an older, stooped gentleman, holding shakily to a cane. They seemed to know one another.

"I guess your dad used to go here," said Daniel with a chin point in Dr. Knight's direction.

"Yes," answered Meriwether, "He told me that this is

where he and my mom got married. This was probably their church, and you know what?" the idea had just occurred to her, "I bet they got your gran coming here too!"

"Nice bit of deduction there, Sherlock," grinned Daniel mischievously.

"Elementary, my dear Dr. Watson," quipped Meriwether, blushing despite herself at having called Daniel *dear*. A nervous giggle escaped her throat, but he didn't seem to notice. Reverend March was ascending the steps up to the dais, and after a few seconds of last minute bustling, a hush fell over the congregation.

The day had turned hot and sticky while they were sitting in church. Reverend and Mrs. March invited them to lunch at the rectory, and they graciously accepted, eager to prolong the long walk back to town. The March home was a study in minimalism. Everything in the house appeared to have a purpose, and nothing was set about merely for decoration. The walls, however, were hung with black and white photographs of mission trips the couple had taken to Africa and China, and several watercolor paintings of St. Mary's, Iffley Village, and Oxford's many universities. Meriwether commented how lovely she thought the drawings were, and with a little open-armed bow, Reverend March smiled benignly, "My hobby."

Mrs. March chimed in instantly, "Don't be modest, now, Alan." Then to Meriwether, "He does postcards, and his paintings sell in a little shop on the High Street called 'South Winds'. . . you should go in there sometime. He's really quite good..." she ended with a beaming smile at her clearly embarrassed husband. Meriwether was surprised (to say the least) at this outburst, which had the effect of greatly improving her opinion of Mrs. March, whatever her resemblance to Aunt Phil.

"And what about your photographs, dear?" returned Reverend March, putting his arm around his wife's waist. "She's been featured in *The Morning Evangelist* several times, but she's much too modest to ever tell anybody that."

They smiled affectionately at one another for a moment; then Mrs. March turned purposefully toward the kitchen, strapping her apron over her church clothes. "Well . . . lunch isn't going to make itself!"

After they ate and visited some more, Reverend March offered to drive the lunch party back home -- the weather could not seem to make up its mind -- the hot and sticky day now a steady summer rain.

"Hope to see you again soon, Peter," waved a smiling Reverend March as the four climbed out of his battered little car and huddled underneath an umbrella Mrs. March had loaned them.

"Yes, well . . . good to see you again Alan...Thanks again for the lunch," responded Dr. Knight noncommittally.

Reverend March appeared un-phased, "Effie, Daniel, Meriwether . . . it was a pleasure."

"Thank you, Reverend March," replied Meriwether, backing away from the curb.

"Yeah, thanks!" waved Daniel.

"Thank you for the ride, dear," said Mrs. Doone. "I look forward to next Sunday."

"The Lord's Day is always something to look forward to!" Reverend March's tiny car lurched forward with a quick burst of speed, kicking water up with its tires, and made a screeching U-turn -- narrowly avoiding an oncoming lorry. Dr. Knight, Daniel, and Meriwether all winced, and Mrs. Doone covered her eyes with a sharp intake of breath, but Reverend March waved cheerfully out the driver's side window as he sped along Abingdon Road, back to the sleepy little village of Iffley.

Dr. Knight grinned and shook his head, ". . . always was a crazy driver . . . . "

Mrs. Doone unlocked the front door and shook out the umbrella as the slightly damp quarto made their way into Dr. Knight's study. "So, what do you think?" wondered Dr. Knight, plopping down into a large leather arm chair. Meriwether told her dad what she suspected about the carvings -- that they were never meant to be identical, and Dr. Knight agreed with her hypothesis.

"Well, and I'm glad I'm not the only one who couldn't see those symbols properly," stated Mrs. Doone as she busied herself lining everyone's wet and discarded shoes along the hearth. "I thought for a minute I was getting old!" Meriwether, Daniel, and Dr. Knight shared a quick look, and Daniel had to bite his lip to keep from sniggering.

Recovering a bit, Daniel asked, "So what's the plan now?"

They all looked at each other blankly. After a moment, Meriwether pushed herself up from the squashy sofa saying, "I guess its back to the box. It's the only clue we've got." She climbed the stairs to her room, retrieved the box from its hiding spot in the top of her armoire, (she kept changing the location . . . just in case) and brought it back downstairs to the study. They spent the rest of the afternoon studying the carvings.

Mrs. Doone was the first to beg off, muttering she had the tea to attend to. Dr. Knight retired to his studio soon after, leaving it to Meriwether and Daniel. Finally, Daniel stood to go. It was getting dark and his mom would be expecting him. Meriwether continued to stare at the images until she felt her eyes would cross. Mrs. Doone brought her tea in on a tray, and Meriwether ate without really tasting it. It was here ...somewhere ...she just knew it! But try as she might, she just couldn't see it. Annora's secret, if there really was a secret, was well hidden. At long last, Meriwether drug herself up the stairs and placed the box in the bottom drawer of her desk. She would not give up, but her brain had had about all it could take for one day.

    That night as she slept, Meriwether dreamed a visit to her grandmother in the hospital. They were working on the word jumbles, and Grandmother was looking at her expectantly from behind her jade green spectacles. As Meriwether studied the jumbled up words, the letters on the page melted into symbols. The symbols started to swirl and swim in front of her eyes, and in her dream, Meriwether could make no sense of them ...Presently, however, the turning, swirling symbols began to look familiar. Meriwether cocked her head to one side and squinted at the shapes -- which weren't shapes any more...Once more, they had become letters.

    Meriwether awoke with a start. Flipping on her overhead light, she pulled Annora's box out of her desk drawer and hefted it on to the middle of her bed. She drew her hair back into a hasty pony tail and sat Indian style in front of the box. Meriwether opened the lid to the relief of the woman praying and began to methodically turn the box in her hands while she held her head to one side and squinted at the symbols lining the perimeter, just like in

Meriwether Mystery Emily Beaver

her dream. At first she wasn't sure what she was seeing, but. . . slowly. . . some of the shapes began to reveal themselves as letters, turned this way and that, disguised amid the surrounding symbols.

This was it! This had to be it!

Meriwether hopped up from her bed and grabbed her handy notebook and pen. Quickly returning to her position, she carefully copied down the letters she found hiding amongst the symbols:

E   G   D   F   O   E   Y   H   E   T   O

All chance of sleep long gone, Meriwether set the box aside and stared fixedly at the letters she had written, then turned again to the box to make sure she hadn't left any letters out. After several long minutes of careful study, Meriwether had rewritten the same eleven letters. This time, she was convinced that she hadn't missed anything. Meriwether took a deep breath and rubbed her closed eyelids deeply with her fingertips . . . *you can do this*. Holding the paper out in front of her, Meriwether used her old trick, un-focusing her eyes, allowing the letters to swim about and form the hidden word. . . *G -- o -- d . . . Godfrey? . . . . No, there's no 'R ' . . . maybe Geoff?* (Pronounced Jeff - she'd seen it written that way before in books) . . . *but, no, there's usually another 'F ' . . . of . . . to . . . the . . . eye* ...Small words kept popping out, but no one word would materialize.

Meriwether looked at the paper in front of her where half-thoughts had been copied out by some independent function, and an idea began to forge. *Maybe it's not one*

168

Meriwether Mystery   Emily Beaver

long word, thought Meriwether as she recalled the first Sunday she had gone to church with Mrs. Doone . . . a nod . . . and a whisper . . . "The Eye of God."

169

Chapter Twenty-One

Next morning at breakfast . . . Meriwether was pleasantly surprised to find Daniel already there, ready for another day of sleuthing . . . Meriwether explained to her compatriots what she had managed to decipher. Dr. Knight, Mrs. Doone, and Daniel, all suitably impressed with Meriwether's detective work, leapt excitedly into a discussion about what the clue might mean.

"Well, we'll just have to do some snooping around, I expect," said Daniel at last.

"Yes, well that may be more difficult than you think," cautioned Mrs. Doone. "Virginia keeps a sharp eye out for anything amiss about the building, and Reverend March is no dunce I can tell you."

"No, he's not," replied Dr. Knight. "Actually, I don't think we should try to keep our mission from them any longer. I'll phone Alan this afternoon . . . tell him what's up. We'll need his knowledge of the church if we're going to get any further with this."

To Meriwether, this was good news. Little white lying to the preacher and his wife was never something she had been particularly comfortable with anyway.

That evening at dinner, the Knights had two visitors. Reverend and Virginia March joined the residents of #240, plus Daniel, in the cramped bit of space they called a dining room.

"Aha!" exclaimed Mrs. March as Dr. Knight brought their tale to an end. "I knew you all were up to something yesterday!"

Rev. March's eyes twinkled behind his spectacles, "She did, you know. Should've worked for Scotland Yard, this one."

"Yes, well it was the best I could do on the spot," smiled Dr. Knight as he dug into the trifle Mrs. Doone and Meriwether were serving. "So, what do you think?"

Rev. March paused, lingering over a mouthful of trifle. "I think that you should invite us to dinner more often. This trifle is delicious, Effie."

Mrs. Doone actually blushed . . . something Meriwether had never seen her do. For a moment, Meriwether could imagine her as she must have looked years ago, as a young woman, blushing for her Robert. "My grandmother's recipe . . ." she lilted. "Top secret, you know."

"Oh, the recipe wouldn't do me any good!" chuckled Rev. March. "Virginia won't let me eat this sort of thing at home . . . . Just make it for me, say, a hundred more times, and I'll be satisfied."

"A hundred more servings of this and she'll be bringing one to your funeral," quipped Virginia. "Seriously, Effie, this *is* divine. Don't know what you'd have done without her, Peter."

"Neither do I, Virginia. Meriwether and I would probably be making ourselves fat on fast food right now . . . that or spearing Vienna sausages out a can. Not that I mind Vienna sausages, mind you . . . absolute life-savers on a dig," he winked.

They agreed to meet evening after next, to give the Reverend a chance to comb some of the church records and documents he was privy to. Mrs. March, meanwhile, would give the ancient church the *once over*, keeping a sharp eye out for any irregularities that hitherto had gone unnoticed. The Marches assured Dr. Knight and Meriwether that their secret was safe with them, and Meriwether could not help but be hopeful that with their help, they would indeed find the De Braose treasure, or whatever it was that Annora had concealed so long ago.

Truthfully, Meriwether did not care what they found. Jewels would be exciting, but any findings must be turned over to a museum . . . the Ashmolean, probably. Meriwether had no greed for gold -- or fame, for that matter. Getting her picture on the front page of the newspaper held little appeal. The fun of it all was the searching, and along with searching, the finding. She daydreamed about the satisfaction she would feel in putting foot to shovel and forcing down on something hard . . . of hefting cut stone from ancient wall to reveal the hidden compartment within.

She had to keep reminding herself that the chances that they would find anything at all were very slim. Her father and the Marches might search for a year and not find a thing . . . *if only they don't find it without me*, she thought, *then I could bear it*. It might become a summer ritual . . . searching for Annora's lost treasure. Yes, she could take consolation in that possibility -- but still she dreamed. . . .

Warm, close air hung thickly in the dusky sky, and long shadows loomed across the hushed grounds of St.

Mary's. From Church Way, Meriwether could see the lighted windows of the yellow-stoned houses that lined the walk; houses that had witnessed the passage of many centuries.... If only they could speak! But as they turned the corner of the church to approach the West Door, all trace of the outside world vanished. At the same time, right on cue, the sky darkened perceptibly. They approached in silence. Meriwether, straining her eyes, could just make out two figures standing in the shadows of the Door. Despite the humidity, Meriwether shivered -- then promptly chastised herself for being so silly.

"Alan."

"Peter."

The men greeted one another in low tones as Rev. March took a great key from his pocket, unlocked the venerable doors, and held them open for Dr. Knight, Meriwether, Daniel, and Mrs. Doone. The blackness inside the church was almost complete. They stood huddled in the entry, afraid to move until either their eyes adjusted or some source of light was introduced into the gloom.

"Let me just find the light switch here," whispered Rev. March, his fingers fumbling along the wall over Meriwether's head.

"There's no need to whisper, dear," spoke Mrs. March in similarly diminished tones.

"Oh, yes. You're right of course, my love," his fingers found the switch and sconces lining the doors going in and out of the baptistry sprang to life. "This is all a bit *cloak and dagger*, isn't it?" he smiled, looking almost boyish in jeans and tennis shoes. "Have a seat," he proffered, motioning toward some cushioned benches flanking either side of the Door, "and I'll tell you what I've come up with."

They all dutifully complied, Meriwether, her father, and Daniel on one bench -- Mrs. Doone and Virginia March on the other.

"What I've gathered together," began Rev. March, "comprises the majority of what we know about Annora and the other anchoresses of her time." He pulled a yellow legal pad out of the battered leather attaché case he carried and set the case down on the stone floor with a thump. "I've taken the liberty of whittling the information down somewhat. Since we began to renovate the cell, Annora has become a sort of obsession with me. I never dreamed it would all come in so useful . . . forgive me if I get a bit carried away.

"First, let me begin by saying, that by choosing the life of an anchoress, Annora gave up all direct contact with the outside world. She was not allowed to leave her apartment and could only speak to visitors through a small window located on the outside wall of her cell. Another interior window enabled her to view the chancel and listen to services. She was attended by maids who cooked for her and looked after her, and they were able to leave the cell . . . run errands . . . bring news from the outside world. If there is a treasure . . . if something has been hidden all these years, I believe we can assume one of three things: either Annora chose a spot within her cell as a hiding place, broke her vow and left her cell to hide it, or entrusted one of her handmaidens to hide it for her."

"So do you believe she commissioned the box, containing the clue to the whereabouts of the treasure, from Henry III?" asked Dr. Knight.

"That is another mystery, isn't it?" replied Rev.

Meriwether Mystery — Emily Beaver

March, raising one eyebrow. "Again, there is no clear cut answer. It is possible that he was in on the secret. It is also possible that, through the handmaiden, direct instructions were delivered to the craftsman.

"I'd like to take you all into the cell so that you can get an idea of the type of life Annora led. The actual walls collapsed centuries ago. Other than the Church records, very little evidence of her life here remains. We've done our best to reconstruct the area using information from the record and the dimensions and set-up from similar existing cells...Keep in mind our clue, "The Eye of God", a reference to the window above you. Annora could not see The Eye from her small window . . . again, another mystery." As he spoke, Rev. March motioned them to follow him, flipping on lights as they went along. "The villagers are accustomed to my nighttime poking about," he explained. "I do not think the lights will alarm anyone."

They all filed down the center aisle of the sanctuary, "These arches above us echo the arches on the West Door," explained Rev. March. "They represent a gateway into the holiest area of the church, the chancel, which contains the altar."

"That's what Annora could see from her room, right?" observed Meriwether.

"Yes, that is correct. What we now call the chancel was added on in the 13th century and might even have been under construction during Annora's confinement here, but this area," motioning in front of him, "the choir, was the original chancel." He led the group out a side entrance, an entrance Meriwether had noticed before because it faced Church Street. "The only way to enter Annora's chamber is from the outside."

They stepped out into the pitch, for it was now completely dark, and felt their way down a broad stone stair - holding on to one another's shoulders and elbows, more for moral than physical support.

"Creepy, ain't it?" whispered Daniel in the back of Meriwether's ear. Again, Meriwether shivered into the night. No other response was necessary.

"I unlocked the door earlier for convenience," said Rev. March as he held the door open to the cell and ushered them all in. Shrouded in utter blackness, the chamber was darker even than the night. They crowded into the small room, silent and stiff, like strangers standing awkwardly in an elevator.

Ill at ease, they waited...

At last, the heavy wooden door closed resolutely behind him, Rev. March struck a match. The small bit of illumination immediately bolstered their confidence, and they all began to relax as he shuffled about the room, lighting the candle sconces spaced evenly along the square walls. The final effect was not unpleasant. Light flickered and danced on the newly hewn stone. Meriwether extricated herself from the knot in the center of the cell and began to move about - trying to get a feel for what it must have been like for Annora - to know that you were, at last, safe . . . but that you could never, ever leave.

A small cot, made up with plain white linen, resided along one wall -- on the opposite wall, a simple wooden table and chair. Set into the far wall, the wall that connected the cell with St. Mary's was cut a low window shuttered with a slatted wooden door. Beneath the window was a meager cushion, for kneeling, and underfoot woven mats covered - not stone - but earthen floor. In the center of the floor lay a stone slab . . . edges rounded with time and exposure.

Rev. March noticed her looking at it. "The stone was placed to remind Annora of her own death. A sort of 'catalyst for contemplation', if you will. That, and the viewing window, is all that remain from the original cell."

"She . . . she's not b-buried there is she?" sputtered Daniel.

Rev. March smiled. "No, Daniel. She's buried in the churchyard . . . I can take you out to look at it, if you like," he added with a mischievous twinkle in his eye.

"No thanks!" responded Daniel, wide-eyed.

Rev. March chuckled, then to Meriwether he held out his arm, palm open, in the direction of the little window, "Please . . . ."

Meriwether took her place beneath the window. Daniel, Dr. Knight, Mrs. Doone, Reverend, and Mrs. March milled about the room -- studying the slab, discussing various theories -- but Meriwether could not hear them. All of a sudden, she **was** Annora . . . kneeling in isolated devotion.

With timid fingers she reached up and pulled back the little door. Instead of a clear view to what had then been Annora's view of the altar, Meriwether found herself looking through an ornate iron mesh screen. Even this glimpse to her world had been obscured. Rev. March was right. She could not see The Eye.

Meriwether frowned. If Annora could not even see the window from her view into the chancel, what could the clue possibly mean? Was it a clue at all? Were they chasing shadows? Perhaps the letters that had been so carefully carved and concealed were, in fact, but an artful reference to the place Annora had chosen to live out the remainder of her life. Maybe there was no treasure.

With a sigh, Meriwether prepared to share her doubts with the others. She placed her hands on the sill for support from her kneeling position, her fingertips bearing the pressure of her rising. Once again, Meriwether felt a forcible connection with her ancestress. Annora must have arisen from her meditations in just this way. Instinctively glancing down at her splayed fingers, Meriwether noticed the faint and miniscule outline of a carved symbol tipping her left ring finger.

A small cry escaped her throat as she sank back to her knees.

"What is it? Did you find something?" her father was instantly by her side.

Meriwether was nervous with excitement. "I . . . I don't know. There's something here. I need more light . . ."

"More light!" ordered Dr. Knight to no one in particular as he peered over Meriwether's shoulder, attempting to make out the shape swimming enigmatically in the far from adequate candlelight.

Daniel pulled a small flashlight from his jeans pocket, and kneeling down beside Meriwether, shone the clear beam directly onto the symbol.

"It's an eye," gasped Meriwether.

Chapter Twenty-Two

Two seconds later, all six occupants of the small chamber were bunched up, craning for a better look at the eye.

"The eye of God sees all. He is the great revealer of mysteries," murmured Rev. March so quietly that Meriwether was not sure, even in such close quarters, anyone had heard him but herself.

"Way to go, Meriwether," Daniel patted her firmly on the shoulder.

"Why, you're a regular sleuth, dear," added Mrs. Doone affectionately.

"I say, well done," agreed Mrs. March.

Anxious to get a move on, Dr. Knight took charge of the situation. "Everyone stand back and let us have a closer look...Not you, Daniel. We need you to hold the flashlight."

The Marches and Mrs. Doone begrudgingly obeyed by taking one somewhat less than generous step back from the proceedings. Daniel repositioned the beam of light, and the search commenced. Meriwether watched as her father's strong, nimble fingers felt deftly along the stone sill for any groove or trigger that might belie a hiding spot.

After a few minutes, he gave up. "You try it,

Meriwether. Maybe your little fingers can detect something that mine have missed."

As gently as possible, Meriwether felt along the rough cut rock. She remembered once hearing that when one sense is taken away, the others become stronger, so she closed her eyes, willing her fingers to find what her father's could not . . . but her fingers failed.

Close to tears, and fighting desperately to hold them back so that Daniel would not see, Meriwether opened her stinging eyelids. The eye stared blindly up at her, well . . . not directly at her, of course. Its permanent aspect was fixed firmly upon the header of the window.

"That's it!" exclaimed Meriwether, a piece of the puzzle shifting into place ... "What does the eye see? . . . ."

Her hands flew to the top of the window, fingers racing tenderly across the stone right above the eye. Something about this bit of rock felt different . . . lighter somehow. It was a decision her hands made all on their own, with seemingly no help at all from her brain. Just as well . . . because if she'd thought about what she doing . . . defacing an almost thousand year old house of God . . . she might not have had the temerity to do it. And so, quite without voluntary thought, her hands grabbed firmly hold of said stone and -- **pulled!**

"Holy smokes!" coughed Meriwether. A cloud of dust and debris crashed from the sill to the floor beneath as the mortar gave way. Meriwether reached gingerly down, digging amidst the rubble. Underneath the hollowed stone lay something small and dark. Meriwether picked up what appeared to be some sort of cloth pouch. She inserted a trembling finger into the top of the enclosure. The decaying string broke away at her touch.

Holding her breath, Meriwether tipped the pouch into her outstretched hand. The contents slid out; their origin unmistakable. Mathilda's emerald and pearl necklace lay coiled in Meriwether's palm like a glittering snake, and loose jewels spilled onto the rush covered ground.

It was all they could do to stop from yelling and whooping aloud enough to bring the whole village running. Needless to say, there was much hugging and congratulating . . . not to mention a little hysterical laughing.

Suddenly, a clear cool voice rent the warm night air like an icy knife. "Brava, Meriwether. What a very clever girl you are . . . and now, if you please, the De Braose treasure . . . ."

She stood before them, bathed in moonlight diffusing from the open doorway . . . dark hair impeccably pulled back, clad from head to toe in basic black. One hand lazily gripped a shining silver pistol; the other slim brown appendage lay outstretched, awaiting its prize.

Meriwether wheeled about, a steely glint in her eye. She would not hand over her booty without a fight.

"I said, now," the woman repeated, reciprocating Meriwether's stare with equal vehemence.

"I see you gave them the slip, Samila," said Dr. Knight in what could have been an affable tone had not his jaws been nearly cemented together with repressed rage. He placed his hand on Meriwether's shoulder, a silent message to remain where she was.

Zanjani smiled her cat that ate the canary smile. "As you are well aware, Peter darling, I am a woman of *many* talents."

The double entendre was disgustingly obvious. Meriwether and Mrs. Doone found one another's' eyes and shared a look of revulsion.

"I repeat, and will not do so again," Zanjani raised the pistol and pointed it directly at Meriwether, "give me the treasure."

Meriwether looked searchingly at her father. Jaw still rigidly clenched, he nodded his assent.

"You'll never get away with this, you know," growled Meriwether, taking a single stiff step toward her nemesis.

"Oh, no?" purred Zanjani, "And who, pray, is going to stop me?"

Meriwether heard a sickening, *Thud!* and watched, speechlessly, as Zanjani fell to the ground in a heap. Behind her limp form, like an Amazon warrior, stood Irene Pleasant, dressed to the nines in high-heeled ankle boots and a short black mini-skirt, sporting a smile as big as Christmas --and a rather large shovel. "That would be me," she beamed.

Chapter Twenty-Three

One week later, Meriwether sat on her bed in the pink and white room and finished her packing. It was time to go back. She smiled to herself as she remembered the events from just a few short days ago. Daniel's mom had been sure they were all up to something, so had followed them to Iffley that fateful night. Hiding in the shadows, she had witnessed another visitor arrive on the scene. Dr. Zanjani never stood a chance.

The police had escorted a bruised and shaken Zanjani into custody; the necklace and loose jewels were turned over to the Ashmolean. Dr. Knight was currently in the process of cleaning them in preparation for a much hyped public debut and was interviewing for a new assistant. Meriwether and crew had gotten their picture in the paper and she had enjoyed -- and endured -- a small bit of celebrity during her last days in Oxford.

Mrs. Doone had found a packing box with lots of Styrofoam peanuts for Meriwether to use in transporting Annora's box back to Grandmother. She would take it as her carry-on.

Meriwether zipped her bag shut and stacked everything neatly against the wall between her bed and the door, then, with a sigh, went down the stairs and into the dining room for her goodbye dinner.

They were all there: her father and Mrs. Doone, Daniel, Irene, and an oily little guy named Ace -- *this must be her boyfriend*, thought Meriwether . . . *no wonder Daniel isn't too impressed*. Reverend and Virginia March rounded out the small party that pushed the limits of the room. Everyone was smiling. Balloons hung from the light fixture above the table and were crammed into every corner. It was beautiful.

After the feasting and merrymaking, Meriwether and Daniel slipped out. They sat on the front stoop, inhaling the fumes of the Lorries that rumbled past in the darkness.

"Nothing like a bit of fresh air, eh?" grinned Daniel.

Meriwether smiled a watery smile. She didn't trust herself to speak.

Daniel elbowed her in the side, "Cheer up, will 'ye? You'll be back before you know it! ...Nothing's going to change, you know," he added quietly.

"Thanks," she said, chin resting on folded arms. She'd finally gotten used to traffic going the wrong way. Would it look backwards when she got back to Texas?

The front door opened, and they were flooded in light from the entryway. "I thought I saw you two come out here." It was Dr. Knight. "Mind if I have a minute, Daniel?"

"Yeah, sure!" Daniel popped up in one agile movement and disappeared into the house.

Dr. Knight took Daniel's place on the steps, mimicking Meriwether's knees up posture. They sat in silence for a few moments. He obviously had something to say, and Meriwether thought she would wait and let him say it.

"I'm coming with you," he said at last.

"What?" Meriwether could not believe her ears.

"I hired a new assistant today. She's a very competent graduate student, and, I believe, more than able to continue with the necessary cleaning and . . . ."

"Did you say you're coming with me?" Meriwether wanted to be sure she had heard correctly before she let herself get too excited.

"Two weeks, starting tomorrow," replied Dr. Knight. "It's not much, but time enough to make amends . . . I hope."

Meriwether threw her arms around her father. "That's great Dad . . . really great. Everything will work out . . . you'll see."

When Aunt Phil met them in Dallas she got quite a shock. Apparently, her errant baby brother had failed to announce his impending arrival. In fact, Meriwether had never seen her aunt so dumbstruck. For a good five to ten minutes, she was quite without anything to say. Meriwether rode in the backseat the whole way. When awake, she chattered aimlessly -- asking about Aunt Phil's kids, her cousins; inquiring after Grandmother; sharing anecdotes from her trip (while skirting some of the more harrowing aspects) -- in an attempt to sever the terse silence that charged between the estranged siblings.

They arrived in Sterling City jet lagged and road weary. It was late, and the capacious house, except for one lone light, was abed.

"Quietly," hissed Aunt Phil as they let themselves in the side door. "Mother will already be asleep. Peter, there should be clean sheets in your closet. I would have had the bed made up if I'd known you were coming." Meriwether couldn't imagine why she was whispering . . . Grandmother's bedroom was a good half mile away.

If Phil was looking for some sort of response, she didn't get one. Too tired to do anything but nod lethargically, Dr. Knight headed for his old room. Meriwether and Aunt Phil, in turn, drifted off to their respective sleeping spots; Meriwether was out as soon as her head hit the pillow.

Chapter Twenty-Four

Next morning, Meriwether awoke to the happy sound of birds chip-chirruping outside her bedroom window. She would have liked to laze about a bit, luxuriating in the delicious crispness of freshly laundered sheets against her bare legs . . . but she was anxious to see Grandmother, and nervous for her father.

Meriwether dressed quickly, breathing in the familiar smell - the one you stopped smelling when you lived there every day - of the home she had known since infancy. She skipped down the hall, running her fingertips along the muted leaf wallpaper; through the dark and curtained den; and across the sun porch, blazing with morning light.

She stopped short at the scene that lay before her. Grandmother sat erectly and perfectly turned out at the gleaming breakfast table. Meriwether's father sat opposite the formidable lady as they shared a cup of coffee -- Annora's box on the table between them. They seemed deep in earnest conversation, and Meriwether hated to intrude, but Dr. Knight had noticed her and - standing up - smiled and motioned her in.

Grandmother turned her head and smiled, "There she is!"

Meriwether approached, placing her cheek against her grandmother's, "Hello, Grandmother," she murmured. Mrs. Knight patted her granddaughter's exposed cheek in a reserved display of familial affection.

"She's forgiven me, Meriwether. I am absolved," declared Dr. Knight with a great smile and shining eyes.

Meriwether looked from her father to her grandmother. Both were beaming, and Meriwether could not resist kissing Grandmother's cheek, then hurrying round to the other side of the table to do the same for her father.

"I knew everything would be all right!" she sang as she returned to Grandmother and took the seat beside her. "I'm so . . . relieved!"

"So am I," puffed Dr. Knight, taking his seat.

"And I," echoed Mrs. Knight. "I was worried you wouldn't accept my apology."

"What?" Dr. Knight and Meriwether exclaimed.

Grandmother took a deep breath to steady herself, and then looked straight into the eyes of her son.

"I always knew it was you who took the box, Peter. And I knew why. I discovered it missing shortly after you left home. I agonized over whether or not to tell your father. He could be a hard man, and he was already angry with you ...In the end, I decided to keep it to myself.

"Several years later we were robbed. Some of my best silver -- your great-great grandmother's, Meriwether -- was stolen, along with a bit of cash and, if you can believe it, a ham from the refrigerator. I simply added the box and its contents to the list of missing items. Philomena guessed the truth, but your father, bless his soul, remained blissfully unaware."

Meriwether Mystery　　Emily Beaver

"So Dad didn't think I was a thief?" asked Dr. Knight, his voice cracking.

Grandmother shook her head.

"All those years . . . wasted," said Dr. Knight in disgust, holding his head in his hand.

Grandmother reached across the table and took his other hand in her own. "We have all paid the price for our stubborn pride. Let this be a lesson to you, Meriwether. Do not make the mistakes we have made."

Just then, a knock came at the side entrance where they had entered last night. Leaving Grandmother and Dr. Knight to it, Meriwether jumped up and raced for the door. Two short raps, pause, then two more could only be one person. Meriwether flung open the door. Holly stood, tall and brown, in the doorway. She had cut her long thin hair into a flattering sun-bleached bob that curved at her jaw line; her deep blue eyes flashed beneath dark lashes.

She grabbed Meriwether up tightly, "I can't believe you're back! You look great!"

"So do you," laughed Meriwether. "I think you've grown a foot!"

"That's what my mom says," she laughed back.

"And I love your hair!"

"Really?" Holly's fingers fiddled nervously with the ends of her shorn locks. "Luke and John are making fun of me. They say I look like a boy."

Meriwether looked at her friend appreciatively and shook her head, "No way, absolutely not!"

They shared another laugh and a hug, and then Holly slid her arm in Meriwether's and said, "Wanna ride bikes? . . . . I have sooo much to tell you . . . ."

Meriwether smiled up at Holly and answered,

Meriwether Mystery   Emily Beaver

"Yeah, me too."

The End

Meriwether Mystery Emily Beaver

Meriwether Mystery   Emily Beaver

Meriwether Mystery   Emily Beaver

...coming in August, 2008

from The Cave at Goat Mountain

    Lightning flashed far away in the night sky, and the distant rumble of thunder broke the stillness of the gloom. The wind began to pick up, whipping locks of disheveled hair against her face.

    Abel had been right. The storm was coming.

    Meriwether pulled the dark hood of her poncho closer about her head as tiny bullets of rain pelted suddenly from the heavens. She shivered as long, jagged fingers of illumination reached across the horizon, an eerie strobe of the twisted mesquites and sparse hills surrounding their camp.

    The campfire struggled and flickered wildly in the wind, and much as she hated to, Meriwether doused the flames with dirt. She would not be responsible for a grass fire. The land was parched, and a small smattering of rain would not stop a hungry fire, gorging itself on dry grass and summer scorched brush.

    Longingly, she imagined Holly -- safe and dry in her nice warm bed. Then she thought of her father and Dr. Lymon, fast asleep in the tent. *I could wake them*, she thought. But no, what could they do? It was just a thunderstorm, and she had agreed to first watch.

    Despite herself, Meriwether began to think about

the stories Abel had told around the campfire earlier that night. Stories steeped in legend . . . of mythical creatures still rumored to roam the land. She knew he had been trying to scare her, but something about the look in his eyes when he spoke of the great bird made her wonder if he didn't believe his own tales.

"I have never seen the great one," he had said, "but my father swore it was real. He saw the storm rider once, as a hijo in Old Mexico. Some say he never lands . . . that he soars on the wind and rides the storms, snatching his prey from the sky. None are safe from such a one as this. It is said that if you see the thunderbird, and live to speak of it, you will be blessed with good luck all the days of your life."

An odd feeling of foreboding crept over Meriwether and a shiver inched up her spine. She tugged at the billowing ends of the poncho, securing them firmly about her slight frame, and watched the gathering storm.

A fork of lightning rent the sky right above her. The light cast from the flash illuminated a great shape gliding in from the north.

It was a bird.

Meriwether's heart went into spasms and her throat felt as if a large pill were stuck at its base. She tried to reason with herself as the thunder, catching up with its source, crashed all around her.

Just an eagle, she told herself. *Calm down. Don't freak out.*

Then another flash broke across the blackness. Not a hundred feet above her, the looming shape of an enormous winged creature soared on the currents of the storm.

Meriwether Mystery Emily Beaver

It was the size of a small airplane.

Meriwether held her breath and willed herself not to move – when her first reaction was to dive into the mouth of the tent behind her. The majestic bird sailed silently over her. It might have been her imagination, but Meriwether thought she could feel the whoosh of him on top of the gusting wind.

He was gone as fast as he appeared. By the time lightning webbed across the sky again, he had disappeared into the night.

Meriwether Mystery — Emily Beaver

Books in the series:

"The Recluse of Iffley Village"
published January 2008
for readers aged 9-14
ISBN: 978-1-933660-42-4
Clothbound
Retail $18.95

"The Cave at Goat Mountain"
release date August 2008
for readers aged 9-14
ISBN: 978-1-933660-43-1
Clothbound
Retail $18.95

"The Ghost of Meriwether Manor"
release date January 2009
for readers aged 9-14
ISBN: 978-1-933660-44-8
Clothbound
Retail $18.95

"The Curse of the Heretic Queen"
release date August 2009
for readers aged 9-14
ISBN: 978-1-933660-45-5
Clothbound
Retail $18.95

Meriwether Mystery & Emily Beaver

Author Biography

Emily Beaver, first time author, lives in Snyder, TX and teaches Theatre Arts at the local junior high.

She and illustrator/cowboy husband A.J. are natives of West Texas. Together, they have three young children.

After graduating from Abilene Christian University in 1996 with a degree in English literature, Emily taught for three years; then stayed home with her children for seven.

In the fall of 2005, she began writing her premier novel, *The Recluse of Iffley Village*, written as the first in a series of Meriwether Mysteries targeting adolescents, ages 9 to 14.

Writing and publishing a novel represents the culmination of a lifelong dream for Emily. Always an avid reader, she is delighted to share stories of her own with a new generation of young readers.